FAME AND
FORTUNE
AND MURDER

Book Three: The Fiona
Fleming Cozy Mysteries

PATTI LARSEN

Cover design by Christina G. Gaudet.

www.castlekeepcreations.com

Edited by Jessica Bufkin.

ISBN-13: 978-1-988700-11-3

CHAPTER ONE

T HERE WAS JUST SOMETHING spectacular about a hot latte and a deliciously sunny April morning that stirred my optimism. Not that I had anything to complain about, really, but the beaming sunshine and perfectly roasted and sugared aroma of fresh coffee mixed with the smiling relief of small town residents recently released from the depressing gray of winter put an extra bounce in my step.

Not just mine, either. As I passed through the glass doors of the most yummy smelling place in all of Reading, Vermont—who didn't adore the scent of well-brewed Colombian?—and into the warm and welcoming arms of spring, I nodded with excellent humor to everyone who returned the grin I shared like we had some secret we'd long been keeping to ourselves and were only now beginning to pass around.

Even the air smelled of new beginnings, that particularly heavenly mix of freshness and damp earth mingling with the scent of crushed pine needles washing down from the mountains seemed to melt away the misery of the last three weeks. Now, allow me to be clear. We hadn't just come through Armageddon or six snowstorms in a row or even a hurricane. Instead, the twenty-one days of pretty much incessant rainfall had turned our entire quaint town into a damp and mildewing mud ball. I'd given up on any chance of getting into the garden at Petunia's, my bed and breakfast, before summer at that rate, each and every morning dragging me deeper into the gloom of misty patheticness fed by temperatures far too mild to even make snow.

And thanks to the loss of cold weather, tourism dried up to the point I only had one set of guests in my normally packed house, a pair of patiently kind grandparents who'd come from Florida to enjoy spring in Vermont. At least now they'd be able to emerge from their hideout in the carriage house Blue

Suite and explore town instead of spending endless hours playing our worn down Monopoly that I was positive was missing Boardwalk.

I passed the new statue that had been erected just a week ago, the rain keeping most residents away from the ceremony, though the bronze gleamed nicely in the sunny day that was today. I still wondered why Olivia Walker, our illustrious and driven mayor, worked so hard to push through the design that now towered over the center of Main Street like some kind of out-of-place colossus. It wasn't like our town needed the twelve-foot tall swashbuckling monstrosity that was her rendering of Captain William Reading, the legendary privateer who founded our town on his own last name with help from his cabin boy, Joseph Patterson.

There weren't any Readings left, though the Patterson family was still around and kicking and making lives miserable from time to time. In fact, one of their disowned daughters, Aundrea, was a friend of mine and a deceased grandson the victim of a murder just two months ago at the White Valley Ski Lodge.

I had heard the Pattersons fought Olivia over the statue and that she'd only won because she had the clout of the full town council behind her thanks to her successful track record. I guess I could see why that old family might want to forget they came from common stock, their famous ancestor barely more than a scruffy kid, some almost but not quite pirate's sidekick.

Petunia grunted next to me as she trotted along, doing her best to keep up and distracting me from Olivia's new twist on town tourism. The legend of Captain Reading never really made sense to me. From what I understood, despite semantics, Reading was little more than a hoarder at the end, gathering his treasure and carting it inland to some hidden location no one ever uncovered. Whispers of that lost hoard and even his brigantine ship, the *Darkling Dragon*, hiding somewhere in the surrounds of Reading were about as common as the idiots who wasted their time looking for it. And found bupkis.

Maybe Olivia was trying to tap into the treasure hunter set? Or, more likely, I smelled a shot at a reality show. She had her head up Hollywood's butt enough tapping into some of Reading's more famous residents that a project like a show based on nothing might just be on her radar.

As long as my rooms stayed full and I wasn't sucked into the drama, I was happy to let her do her thing.

Petunia groaned while we continued on, pausing to scratch one ear with an awkward hind leg before huffing forward. I'd spent the winter trying to regulate her diet and get her off the treats and sugar my best friend, Daisy, and own traitor mother had been sneaking her. But it was apparent either the pug named after my inherited business was finding ways to steal extra food or the two older ladies who worked for me were ignoring my orders not to give the dog anything not on her approved list. The post-it note stuck to the big stainless steel fridge had gone missing lately, I noticed, so I had a feeling it was the latter rather than the former.

"Don't think that donut hole you just ate is going to be a regular occurrence," I said, unable to resist the offer when the perky young woman handed over the sugary confection. Petunia's pathetic expression and bulging eyes showing the whites tweaked my heart strings and, I guess, the lovely day made me generous.

Petunia didn't even look up at me, likely plotting her next opportunity to bully someone into giving her food that made her flatulent. It wasn't so much her round belly that concerned me as it was her unfortunate habit of farting on me in her sleep. My attempt to kick her off the bed had failed completely and she'd been curled up next to me every night since I gave in. But if she was going to keep expelling that level of gas it was quite possible I'd go to bed one night and just never wake up.

Toxic pug gas slayed.

I skipped around a small stack of pylons and a long, low barrier of white painted lumber while my deputy cousin unloaded more of the same from the back of the sheriff's pickup. I beamed at Robert Carlisle, not because I adored him. Quite the opposite. I couldn't stand the wretched little piece of loathing with his seventies-esque bush of a black mustache or his pompous superiority that he got to be a cop and I didn't or his growing beer belly and hideous leer he liked to aim at any woman under the age of fifty. And the feeling was mutual, though none of the previous applied. I was sure Robert had his own list of things about me he despised, but I was positive his number one reason for hating my guts was the fact I was the daughter of former sheriff John Fleming and he would never, ever be.

No, I grinned and waved out of sheer delight at his less than enthusiastic expression as he grunted his way through hefting a rather heavy looking barricade onto the sidewalk.

"Exercise is good for you," I said as I kept going without offering to help.

"Your ass could use some lately, Fanny," he shot after me.

CHAPTER TWO

H E DID *NOT JUST* call me fat and Fanny in the same sentence. I spun back, good mood turned to snarling anger, and found Deputy Jillian Wagner smiling at me, shaking her head. Once I discovered Jill couldn't stand Robert either, I'd invited her over for coffee and her best advice hit me with that smile.

Do not engage the troll.

Instead, I paused next to her and completely ignored my cousin who glared at us. Jill took a break, her blonde ponytail tucked into the collar of her khaki uniform button up, white t-shirt showing at her collarbone. Nice to know another woman about my height, especially in Reading where everyone seemed to lean toward the petite side. While 5'7" wasn't gigantic, I sometimes felt like I towered over other women, including my elderly employees, Mary and Betty Jones. Made me feel a bit awkward.

"You staying around for the parade?" Jill's voice always surprised me, sweet and light, and from what I heard she was a hell of a soprano.

Oh, crap, right. I'd forgotten the parade. On purpose. "Ah," I said, looking down at my latte.

She laughed. "Gotcha. Gardening?" She sounded wistful.

I beamed a smile. "Can't wait to get into the beds now that the ground is drying out some. I might transfer some of the bushes but for now I'm going to clean up and prep for planting." If any of my old friends from my five years living in New York City could have heard me they'd have fallen off their designer platforms and spilled their own expensive and impossible to order coffees. A lot had changed since my Grandmother Iris died and left me Petunia's. Including two murders and a secret trail of clues that led me to a broken music box I was in the process of having restored.

"I'll pop over when I get the chance if that's okay?" Jill lifted a pile of orange cones from the back of the truck. "I'd love to get slips of the two bushes near the front steps if that's still all right?"

I grinned, nodded. "I'll be home all weekend," I said. "Avoiding the fanfare."

She wrinkled her nose, freckles coming together under her blue-gray eyes. Not many people I knew looked that good without makeup, her naturally dark lashes so thick I felt envy every time I looked at her. "Wish I could join that club," Jill said. "But it's all hands on deck this weekend."

I wasn't surprised. "Has Olivia been driving Crew nuts?" Ever since the weather turned and our tourist numbers with it our dear Mayor Walker had been slowly losing her mind. Her push to attract visitors had, so far, created a wave of new business for Reading and I was frankly impressed by her determination. While the whole grow or die mentality gave me the creeps, I couldn't complain about the benefits to my bank account.

But as I looked around the busy main street of the place she'd coined the "cutest town in America," I wondered if these past few weeks of quiet weren't a good thing. It had been nice to relax a little, put my feet up, get to some projects requiring my attention without feeling like I had to hurry or scurry or fudge the edges because I just didn't have time.

There was something to be said for a break in the crazy, especially with summer coming. And this weekend's activities were bound to stir things up again.

"Have Willow and Skip arrived yet?" The focal points of today's parade, Reading's most famous citizens lived in Hollywood full time. But that didn't stop Olivia from shamelessly badgering the A-list star and her football hero husband to promote our town. Which, I thought, they'd done so far with grace and thoughtfulness, part of the reason Olivia's campaign to increase tourism had worked out so well. But this weekend's commercial filming following the pomp of a parade for the happy couple was just a bit much for my stomach.

Thus hiding in the garden in the sunshine and letting the rest of Reading deal.

"I think so," Jill said. "The sheriff and the mayor were driving to the airport to meet them at 9AM, so I assume they're back by now." Likely staying at the White Valley Ski Lodge in the penthouse suite. I personally preferred to avoid the place since almost dying on Valentine's Day and helping solve two murders. But it was a beautiful spot and the perfect refuge for the famous pair.

"Have fun," I said, waving to Jill and tossing my long, auburn hair at Robert who snarled back.

Petunia grumbled about walking as she always did, pausing now and then the two and a half blocks to the B&B just to see if I'd stop and pick her up. Which I refused to do.

"Maybe we both need more exercise," I said. Refused, of course, to believe Robert's cruel comment was anything but crap while a tiny part of me whispered I had been enjoying Betty's cooking a lot lately, not to mention my mother's amazing fare and hadn't I spent the winter working but not working out...? "That's it. We both need to shift our habits. What do you say?" Whether true or not— suck it, Robert—I missed my daily runs in the city. Time to take that up again.

Petunia didn't seem all that enthusiastic. I should have adopted a Labrador.

I looked up as I rounded the corner of Booker Street, heart stuttering while my smile faded and my lovely day of nothing but puttering in the garden took a massive turn for the oh crap now what. My normally quiet street, the odd car lining the sidewalks even when we were fully booked, now looked like a war zone. By the time I forced my sneakered feet past the stretch limo and the giant white van with the camera equipment, cables and lights and other things I couldn't comprehend snaking and looming their intrusion on my life and the three hulking men in dark suits and earbuds with plastic wires running into their collars, I had a horrible, horrible feeling I wasn't in Kansas anymore.

Nope, I was in Reading, Vermont. Cutest town in America.

My desperate need to explain this mess away disappeared with the sudden appearance of Olivia bustling from my front door, hurrying down the steps and to my side where she stopped with a deep scowl and a determined look on her face. One hand lifted to grasp my elbow as she leaned in and hissed the following.

"The lodge has a gas leak and you're all I have. So live with it." She beamed then, leaning away, voice rising to politician volume while I gaped at her. "Petunia's is the perfect place to house our special guests and staging ground for our parade. Historic and distinctly Reading, it's been a landmark in our sweet little town for decades, a favorite of both

Willow and Skip since their childhoods." Wait, what? "I just know our visitors will love their time staying here and the nostalgia it will resurrect for them." She tucked one arm around my shoulders, her dark red suit making me think of blood while I tried desperately to come up with something to say to stop this train wreck from happening. "Thank you so much to Fiona Fleming for being our most gracious host."

Wait, that sounded like a speech, didn't it? I looked away from her to find she'd been speaking to a camera. Of course she had and I stood there and stared at it like an idiot struck by lightning.

I knew then, like it or not, I was now a part of whatever Olivia had planned.

CHAPTER THREE

WE STOOD THERE FROZEN for about five seconds, Olivia's nails digging into my arm, until the young woman behind the lens looked away from the viewer with a thumbs up.

"We're out," she said before ambling away, the complicated looking camera rig she wore over her jeans and t-shirt more from a science fiction novel than a film shoot.

Olivia released me and spun to face me, hand now firmly grasping my wrist, those same oval nails painted matching red to her prim suit carving little crescents into my flesh, all pretense vanished as panic flashed on her face.

"They're stuff is already moved in," she said. "But there's a couple in the carriage house. You need to get them out *now*." She almost panted with anxiety. "Thank god you're empty already or this would have been a disaster bigger than it already is."

"Thanks a lot," I said, jerking my arm out of her grasp. "And who gave you permission to just take over my B&B? Don't tell me I owe you, Olivia." My turn to be fierce, jaw jutting like I knew it did when my temper flared. More my burly ex-sheriff dad than my petite mom, but all redhead. My stomach knotted around aggression as I managed to speak again without choking the mayor. "My services in February have paid that debt in full and then some."

For once she didn't argue, the very real fear in her eyes softening my anger somewhat, leaving irritated frustration behind. "Please, Fee," she said. "I'm asking, okay?" A quick glance cast over her shoulder and a flash of a smile ended with her leaning even closer. "I'll owe you one this time."

Well now. The idea of Olivia Walker being in my debt sounded good, actually. And I *was* empty. All but for the poor Johansens. "I can't just kick out my paying guests." I flinched. "Tell me I'm not volunteering my place for this?"

Hey, no judging. Moncy talked in this town.

"Of course not," she huffed quickly, visibly offended and the last of my anger faded away. "You should know by now I'm a proponent of small business, Fiona Fleming. The town of Reading was going to pay the lodge for accommodations. Those funds will go to you."

I didn't have any new guests for at least a week, so I was out of objections. "Fine," I said. "But you're explaining to the nice couple in the Blue Suite why they have to hit the pavement." Olivia's relief was a wash of pink across her olive skin. "But," I said, "no divas, no drama and if anyone does any damage, you're liable." I really had to have lost my mind. Because with fame and fortune came media and fans and all kinds of other things I couldn't anticipate at the moment. Things I knew would pop up to bite my accommodating self in the ass.

"Done," Olivia said, grabbing my hand this time and jerking me toward the white painted steps to Petunia's. "Now get in here and take care of your guests." Panic gone, she was powerhouse Walker all over again.

My mind stumbled as I did, almost falling in through the front entry of my B&B, while my own anxiety appeared in a flash of what the hell did I just do? I was down a woman, my best friend, Daisy Bruce, good on her word, off trying new career choices. I had, as yet, to replace her because business had been slow. And frankly because I missed her and hoped she'd come back and tell me helping me at Petunia's was her life's purpose.

Maybe I could call her and see if she was free…? The only other person I'd considered for the job, the girl I'd first known as Paisley—then Jenny—turned out to be a multiple murderer and insane to boot, so Daisy was definitely at the top of my hiring chart.

As I blinked into the dimness of the front entry, a familiar face—speak of the angel and she shall appear—beamed at me from behind the podium we used as a front desk. Daisy waved before circling toward me, Petunia heaving herself up for a hug. My best friend lifted the pug into her arms, cradling her on one hip like a toddler, Petunia's favorite position, and kissed her wrinkled brow. But any thought I might have had Daisy was here to rescue me faded at the sight of her blue jeans and plaid shirt tied over her pink tank top, thick hair in two low pigtails over her shoulders, ends curled in perfect coils. Even in casual attire Daisy was the bomb.

The squawk of the walkie talkie hooked to her belt told me she wasn't here for me.

"Isn't it exciting, Fee?" Daisy gushed while scooting sideways to let a tall young man in a dark suit carry a big, black case into the kitchen. I gaped after him but didn't say anything, wondering how the Jones sisters were coping with the intrusion. The two elderly ladies who'd worked first for my grandmother and now for me didn't like change and this was liable to give them both a stroke. "Willow Pink here at Petunia's!"

"Awesome," I muttered, only now noticing the footprints of dirt in my entry carpet, the trailing cables and piles of luggage, the way the banister to the second and third floor had turned into a coat rack and that my front sitting room had somehow converted into a disaster of miscellaneous junk I couldn't identify.

I'm not a neat freak. Or I wasn't until I inherited Petunia's. Mind you, I've never been messy, not really, but a bit of dirt didn't bother me all that much. I have no idea why, as my brain absorbed affront after insult after injury to my place, the temperature inside the foyer seemed suddenly about that of the surface of the sun or why I couldn't breathe except through my open mouth. And that if I didn't get out of there right freaking now I was going to punch someone.

Anyone.

Daisy must have seen the warning signs, because Olivia was long gone and couldn't care less, from all the caution she took making sure my business wasn't treated like a trash heap. My best friend set Petunia down very slowly before grasping my upper arms in her hands and shaking me ever so slightly, gray eyes locked on mine. All I could see while spots danced and I fought for air were the giant pupils, the perfectly made up lashes, the intensity of her worry.

"Fee," she said. "Inhale."

Right. Breathing was important.

"Exhale." She demonstrated and I followed suit. "Again." I nodded, breathed. "Out." And let go of all the stress of this horrifically wretched happenstance. We must have looked like we were practicing Lamaze or something, but I didn't care. Though, when she released me, while my panicked overdrive descent into losing my ever loving mind was over, my temper hadn't faded.

Not even a little bit.

"I'll take care of all this," Daisy said when I opened my mouth to fire off orders to clean up my B&B or so help me *GOD*. Reading my mind again, that Daisy. "I promise. It's my job." She beamed then, curtsied a little. "I'm a P.A., Fee! That's production assistant." She winked then, tipped her hip so her noisy radio was more visible. "Olivia got me the job. Isn't it great?"

She didn't want to know what I thought right at this moment. She really, really didn't. But as she turned and started barking orders to the crew of people lugging things into my place, I stepped past her with Petunia in tow and watched a moment while she quickly and efficiently snapped her whip and sorted out the entry.

I'm pretty sure Daisy's job was entry level. And that a P.A. didn't have the authority to push around some of the people she was bossing in her charismatic and adorable way. But from their startled looks and instant obedience, they knew she didn't know that. Or they thought she was someone they needed to listen to. I didn't care, sagged against the sideboard where the reservation computer hummed softly, and wished I hadn't gotten out of bed this morning.

It would be okay, I knew that. And my reaction to the whole mess startled me. I had no idea I'd become so hidebound and shortsighted, so, well. Old. Crankypants. This was a cool thing, honestly. I was a big Willow Pink fan. Her husband, Skip Anderson not so much, but only because I didn't like football. But I was well aware the two most famous people to come out of Reading had more than enough fans they didn't need me or my approval to be successful.

This was going to be good for our town. I could suck it up, maybe take advantage of the fact they stayed here and call it a win. And stop acting like I was turning into one of the Jones sisters. Shudder.

Daisy smiled and waved to me, making a "ta-da!" gesture of the magician's most lovely assistant while she directed her symphony of equipment. It looked like she had truly found something she loved to do at last. While she'd spent a month waiting tables at the Harp and Thorn, our local Irish imitation tourist trap pub, and another as a barista at Sammy's Coffee, she'd left both with a hangdog expression and come back to me for a bit before trying again. It was nice to see her happy.

Grumble, how could she leave me, mumble, growl, grump.

CHAPTER FOUR

I BUSIED MYSELF WITH non-existent paperwork and had to admit, a short ten minutes later, the foyer looked about as good as it was getting without a solid vacuuming. The crew disappeared out the front door, slamming it shut and I grit my teeth against the sound instead of yelling because I was a good little host. Tempting to start a list and send repairs off to Olivia, but instead I sighed and looked down at Petunia. Still on her leash and in her harness, she lay at my feet, chin on my toes, looking like a fawn sausage tied up to keep her liquid skin from running off.

I wasn't about to admit I'd forgotten her in my huffiness. Besides, she didn't ever seem to care as long as she was with me. Just made the guilt worse, really, not better.

"Snack?" She perked immediately, heaved to her feet. No, I was not above bribing her to assuage my own regrets. I slipped into the kitchen, feeling a bit sick to my stomach in reaction to all the massive emotion I'd gone through the past little while. My expectations and my reality had collided in a massive explosion that I realized I just needed a few minutes and a giant slice of chocolate something to get over.

Betty and Mary, the aforementioned Jones sisters, were nowhere in sight. Since the kitchen was Betty's domain, I was surprised to find her missing, especially at midday. Typically she'd be prepping for afternoon tea, though I suppose she must have assumed that special offering to the townsfolk had to be cancelled considering the pending influx of our special guests. Everything seemed in order, though, so it didn't look like either of them imploded over this turn of events.

I'd take wins wherever I could find them.

I headed for the fridge and the bowl of fresh cut strawberries I kept for Petunia, pausing and staring with my head tilted as someone slipped past the kitchen windows and peeked in before the handle to the back door turned in slow motion. It eased open, the intruder obviously aware they weren't welcome, and I set the bowl down and crossed my arms over my chest, toe tapping the floor in irritation, while Pamela Shard's blonde head popped in. She scanned the room, missing me and my pug entirely, likely thanks to the huge light difference between glaring sunshine and gloomy interior. With a faintly deceptive grin like a kid sneaking out after dark, she slipped inside and softly closed the door behind her. I swear she tiptoed. Seriously.

"Pamela." She jumped when I said her name, squealing in an uncharacteristic show of nerves, grasping at the air before her with both hands, held in front of her to ward off some imagined attack.

"Fee." The one and only newspaper reporter in Reading panted as she laughed out her dose of fear, like my scowl and temper weren't something to be afraid of. Hey, I was a force to be reckoned with, better believe it. "You scared the crap out of me."

"Breaking and entering is a felony," I said like that mattered to her, turning my back on her to fetch the strawberries, feeling like I'd lost my edge or something. Wow, I really was grumpy. Petunia didn't even say hello to Pamela, the word "snack" holding her captive for as long as it took me to utter that suggestion and then get around to feeding her. One track mind, my pug.

I knew how she felt. I really had to shake my inner curmudgeon before it did permanent damage.

"Now, Fee," Pamela said, coming to join me where I sank to a stool with a bowl the one hand, the pug eagerly licking her chops at my feet. The chill of the ceramic felt good on my hand, soothing all of me in a strange way. Familiarity? Okay, now I really did need to shake this off because I refused to fall into routine and mediocrity. "We're friends, right? You won't tell Olivia I'm here?"

That request surprised me. So she wasn't sneaking around to get past me? "She's chased you off?" Weird. "I'd think she'd want local press to have first go."

Pamela shrugged, her bob shining in the low light, gaze flickering to the door to the foyer. "I'm not sure she has that much say in the matter. And besides, she's a bit out of sorts." She laughed like Olivia's discomfort gave her pleasure. "With the gas leak and her plans in a kerfuffle, she's keeping everyone at arm's length." Pamela helped herself to some strawberry before offering a piece to the groaning pug. Petunia licked her fingers, whites of her eyes showing as her fat little rump scooted sideways on the tiles in her excitement.

"Where's the rest of the press?" Yes, that came out snappy. Hmmm. Maybe I needed to just embrace my inner cranky old lady instead of fighting her off.

Pamela's eyes sparkled, lips twisting in delight. "Still at the lodge," she giggled before snorting to a stop. "Such a shame no one told them Olivia snuck Willow and Skip out the back while the crew met us here."

"Us?" My bad mood faded at her obvious cleverness.

"Well, Olivia finally agreed to let me come so I wouldn't shout out our location to the whole lobby," she said. "But when we got here the turncoat sent me off with a warning."

"Which you clearly listened to." I sighed and had a strawberry slice too. Petunia looked up at me like I'd killed her best friend, not sampled her snack. "You do realize I have to live with this situation for as long as it lasts?"

Pamela shrugged. "Just two days," she said, perking my world a bit. "The fabulous duo have to be out by Monday."

"I can't let you in," I said, real regret waking but not enough to cut her slack. Petunia's came first, and that meant keeping Olivia happy. To a point.

Pamela's smile told me she understood. "Just keep me posted if anything juicy comes up." Like her anonymous source during their stay would be construed as anyone *but* me. Which suddenly made me nervous while she turned and headed for the door, waving on her way out.

Damn it, anything she published meant trouble. The whole town would assume I was guilty of spying or sharing secrets or... crap. Just craptastic nastyass grossness on a stick.

Grumpy old lady sounded perfect right about now.

CHAPTER FIVE

THE KITCHEN DOOR SWUNG inward and I tensed, expecting the depressing and judging pair of elderly ladies who ran my place to come galumphing into my presence and demand I do something. Well, Mary, anyway. Betty never, ever talked to me. I wondered sometimes if she even spoke a word to her sister or what reason she might have to hold her silence the way she did.

Who knew? Maybe it was just me.

Instead, a tall and handsome drink of water paused uncertainly just inside the kitchen threshold, his dark hair over his brow, eyes scanning the room, all broad shouldered and narrow hipped and hiding muscles inside that custom suit of his.

Down girl. But it had been almost a year since I slapped my ex-boyfriend, Ryan Richards, for cheating and stormed out of our apartment, leaving New York and my sex life behind. The delectable and frustrating Sheriff Crew Turner and his yummy factor aside, this was the first encounter I'd had with anyone I'd even consider having a drink with who wasn't on a TV show I obsessed over.

The pickings were slim in these here parts.

"Hello?" His voice had that warm, mellow tone of someone who'd had some kind of vocal training. When he spotted me his face lit up, a delicious smile the likes I'd not seen in an age washing over that strong jawline, lifting those full lips, making those high cheekbones stand out under the darkness of his eyes.

"Can I help you?" Wow, impressive. I could speak and didn't sound like I'd just had a stroke from his awesome gorgeousness turning me to jelly. Which I think was a definite possibility if Mr. Yummypants came any closer.

That didn't stop him from moving, did it? Not that I did anything to stop him. He glided his definitely a ten star rating worthy body a few steps toward me, one big hand extended in greeting, eyes never leaving mine in that way that told me I was the center of his particularly fantastic attention.

Ahem.

"You must be Fiona?" He made it a question, still smiling as Petunia, her treat devoured, realized pats were likely in the offering and turned toward his voice. She huffed herself to her feet, trotting to greet him, sinking to her butt next to his shiny black shoes.

There are two kinds of people in this world as far as I'm concerned. The good kind who love animals and small children and treat other people with respect and kindness. Nice folk with souls who actually have the potential for acts of generosity that inspire awe and genuine adoration.

The other kind? I don't have time for them.

His test, like everyone else I encountered while pug encumbered, was Petunia. The way he instantly sank to his haunches from that more than six foot height, how he grinned and made cutesy noises while he gently rubbed her ears until she groaned did a lot more for his image and attractiveness than that expensive haircut and suit.

When he looked up at me again his whole being smiled. "She's adorable," he said. "My mom had pugs. Best dogs ever."

I didn't care if he was married—not from the empty ring finger on his right hand—or dating—move over, sister—that man was mine. Okay, no, I wasn't *that girl* and would never be *that girl*, not after being on the other end of what *that girl* was capable of. But seriously? The Universe had to give me this one. It owed me after the jackass who was Ryan Richards.

"Did you need something?" It was that monotone, standard question or beg him to marry me, so stuffy formal it was.

He didn't seem to mind, standing up and nodding. "I'm part of the security team," he said. "Just checking in. Showing my face. Carter Melnick." He held out one hand again and I stood there, frozen a moment, realizing I still hadn't done him the courtesy of shaking it, because that was the polite thing to do. But wait. He wanted me to touch him and not tear his clothes off? Because I knew he smelled delicious. No I couldn't actually smell him yet, but he had that look about him. He *had* to. Like chocolate probably, mixed with really good coffee and the deep muskiness that made men so tasty you wanted a big, hearty bite.

The second I made contact with his skin and caught his scent I'd be embarrassing the hell out of myself and there'd be no explaining away my patheticness.

Somehow I found myself floating across the tile and taking his hand anyway, as if I wasn't in control of my body. Exactly what I was afraid of, really. But instead of transforming into a lust monkey and hooting my passionate mating cry, I simply shook his hand like a normal person. Go me.

Just as I thought, warm and strong, and his cologne? Oh. My. *God*. Dear Lord, take me now.

My salvation from my devolution into panting patheticness came in the form of another man, this one still handsome but older, and with that kind of jaded and overdone look that told me he'd been in Hollywood too long. His gaze, judging if ever I'd seen it behind dark hazel eyes, swept over me and Carter and then back to me while Petunia marched to his side, sat and growled up at him like he'd offended her by leaving her out of his perusal.

"Mr. Parker." Carter's entire attitude shifted instantly, from kind greeting to professional on the job. "This is Miss Fleming, our host."

"Charming." Disdain had a scent to it, one that curdled my blood. Whoever this jerk face thought he was, no one talked to me like that in my place.

"Fiona Fleming." I shoved my hand in the newcomer's direction and, after observing it a moment, he took it, shook it with the kind of limp disinterest that got my back up all over again. I should have been grateful he rescued me from my hormones. Instead, I just wanted to kick his ass out of Petunia's.

"Julian Parker," he said in his droll and slightly tenor tone, wrinkling his nose—was that makeup? He was wearing *makeup*?—as he perused the kitchen like it offended his precious baby sensibilities, the darling little flower. Snarl. "Willow Pink's manager. I'm here to inspect the premises to ensure things are up to the level of comfort to which she's accustomed."

I smiled, forcing it onto my face. "And I'm here to make sure you're up to my level of guest," I said. "Trust me, you piss me off, Jules? Your asses are out of my B&B and you can all sleep on the sidewalk." Because grumpy had its uses and Olivia could suck it.

"I don't have to take that kind of attitude from someone like you," he said without even the good grace to look angry.

Oh, no he did *not*. "I'm not sure if you're aware," I said, "but you have the following alternatives." I ticked them off on my fingers while Carter stood silently next to me, not caring even a little what he thought at the moment. "Let's see. There's the corporate chain motel on the highway. Oh, but they have a bedbug problem, forgot about that." That made him flinch. "There's the shifty little inn a town over." Cantwell. Yucksville. "Except no one will stay there twice because the owners recycle food and go through guest's belongings when they aren't there." Julian stared at me in utter horror. "Finally, there's always slow death by gas inhalation at the lodge. Or Petunia's. Thing is, I just might be full after all. Depends entirely on you, Mr. Parker."

Standoffs weren't my forte, but damn it, I was a Fleming and my parents didn't raise a pushover. When Julian was the first to look away—albeit to answer his smartphone that rang with an annoying pop tune I couldn't stand—I turned and met Carter's eyes, fully expecting more judgment.

And instead found thinly veiled amusement and trembling lips that clearly hid a smile. Victory? At least the entire encounter with Mr. Manajerk had cooled my jets enough I could focus and function around the deliciousness that was Carter Melnick.

"Very well." Julian's last two words were clear enough, as was his tone. He hung up and glared at me, but I could see he wasn't going to fight me, at least for now. "Ms. Pink is my responsibility," he said. "And I take that job seriously, Miss Denning."

"*Fleming,*" I said.

"Whatever." He slipped his phone into his inside breast pocket. "That being said, we are grateful," that word from between clenched teeth like he'd been instructed against his will to say it, "for your hospitality and I assure you," now a threat, "we won't take up your precious little bed and breakfast's accommodation any longer than we absolutely have to."

Sand strewn. Line drawn.

"Then I guess I'll just have to do my best not to cry my eyes out when your ass walks out my front door." So there.

Julian glared, I glared and, finally, he sniffed, turned and left. Because no man stood against Fiona

Fleming. Or he had somewhere to be. Either way, good riddance.

"He's a troll," Carter said. I turned to find him grinning openly now. "I have no idea why Ms. Pink keeps him around. But she's a softy and he's been with her a long time." He chuckled. "Nice job, by the way. He knows he's stuck and you took the perfect tone. He won't give you any trouble."

"Yeah, I was actually serious," I said. "I'll kick you all out." Well, not him. As the saying went, crackers in bed would never be a deal breaker in Carter's case.

His eyes widened, eyebrows shooting up toward his dark hair. "Even better," he said. "Wow, where have you been all my life?"

Waiting right here for him to come and sweep me off my feet, of course. Silly, silly man.

Our conversation had so much further to go, should have ended with something much more satisfying than an exchange of grins. But the sound of Olivia calling my name from the foyer and the bustle of the arrival of what had to be the main event killed the mood.

I turned for the door only to find Carter beat me to it, slipping around me to hold it open with that smile of his about as shmexy as anything I'd ever seen and softening my temper enough at least I might make it through the next ten minutes without murdering someone.

Maybe. No promises.

CHAPTER SIX

OLIVIA WASN'T ALONE IN the foyer, Julian hovering beside a tall, wafer thin woman in giant sunglasses. I knew who she was, of course, would have guessed she thought herself important regardless of her actual identity. What, in a bad mood all over again despite the hotness following on my heels?

Forgive me my natural redheaded inclination to temper.

Before Olivia could say a word, her beaming smile splitting her painted lips wide, the slender brunette with the tidy ponytail and elegant, if understated, jeans and flowing blouse slipped her glasses free and extended one long-fingered hand toward me, a real smile on her stunning face. Willow Pink was even more beautiful in person, though in a fragile and delicate way that softened my rougher edges as her huge, luminous blue eyes met mine with the kind of genuine authenticity that she was famous for.

"Thank you so much for letting us invade your lovely bed and breakfast, Miss Fleming." She sounded just like she did in the movies, soft but with a level firmness to her tone, practiced and polished. "You're a lifesaver."

I shook her hand, the thin bones feeling odd in my stronger grasp. I knew she was thin—it seemed to be the norm for Hollywood despite advances to the contrary—but I had no idea the old adage that the camera added ten pounds wasn't kidding. She looked like if she sneezed she'd tear apart like tissue paper in a breeze. "Sorry to hear they're having trouble at the lodge." I didn't mean that as a backward anything but winced inwardly as I realized what it sounded like. And after she'd been gracious.

Willow didn't seem to take it the wrong way, though. Instead, she shrugged her thin shoulders under the tidy wool wrap she wore, eyes twinkling in good humor. "I'm just happy to be home," she said, and she actually sounded like she really meant it. "Staying here at Petunia's feels more like Reading than the lodge anyway, so it's made my trip if I'm going to be honest." She turned and laid one hand on Olivia's arm. "No offense meant at all to the beautiful resort Reading can be proud of. But both Skip and I grew up here as you're well aware. And even though my parents moved to L.A. to be near me, I still feel like I belong here in the heart of town, down at the end of Jasmine Street, two blocks over."

"Absolutely," Olivia gushed. There was no other way to describe the enthusiasm she put into that one word.

Before she could say anything else, Willow returned her attention to me. Only then did I realize how quiet it had become in the foyer, like everyone fell utterly silent when she spoke. Not out of need, her volume was fine. I had to admit her natural charisma held me a bit in thrall, too, almost demanding attention as much as she gave it, and naturally, without affectation or command. No wonder she was famous. She could probably talk herself into any role she wanted with pipes like that.

"It's a shame we never met before," she said as if we'd have run in the same circles or something given the opportunity. "I was three years behind you in school. And I left when you were still in college, I think?"

Three years didn't seem that big a gap like it did when I was a senior. "How's L.A. treating a down home Reading girl?"

Willow chuckled, deeper than I expected. "It'll do for now," she said. Inhaled and exhaled with gusto as she looked around Petunia's foyer before spotting my pug and squeaking out a delighted noise, crouching to pat her with great kindness.

Okay, grumpies gone. That joy in her greeting sold me on Willow completely.

"Petunia," she said. Looked up at me. "The Third?" Wistful, sad, without much hope she was right and this was the pug she remembered.

"The Fourth," I said, a bit sorrowful myself when I thought about it. "You knew Grandmother Iris?"

"Did I." Willow kissed the top of Petunia's head, still melancholy but smiling a little. "She and my mother were friends of a sort. Played bridge on Saturday nights, usually here, but sometimes at my house. And Iris would always bring Petunia. I suppose, though, the pug I loved was this darling's predecessor." Willow stood, hugged herself like she was cold suddenly. "I've been gone a long time."

"It's easier than you think to come home," I said with a wry smile. "Almost too easy."

Willow laughed then, the mask of sorrow cracking and falling away. As if on impulse, she hugged me abruptly, the scent of lavender and some kind of soft spice carried on her clothes and in her hair. I embraced her back and, when she let me go, the faint blush on her cheeks registered she might have second guessed her choice.

"Sorry," she whispered. "I'm not normally a hugger. But Iris's granddaughter is an automatic friend of mine."

Clearly from the nervous look in her eyes, the open honesty, she didn't have many real friends. And that feeling I had when she'd acknowledged Petunia? Yeah, it got stronger the longer we talked. I found my temper fading, my grin easy and open as I nodded. Willow Pink might have been a huge movie star, but she was a person first, a Reading girl like me, coming home to a place that meant something to her. Imagine that.

"Willow." Her slimy manager had to go and ruin it, didn't he? Julian's vague smile made my skin crawl. "We really should get you settled."

"Of course. Maybe we can have tea later, Fiona? If you have time?" Willow half turned from me, smiling again as she looked up the stairs. "I have wonderful memories of exploring the rooms in Petunia's. And of your darling grandmother."

"I'd like that," I said. "I can bring it to you when you're ready."

"Thank you." She paused, frowned slightly, head tilting toward the front door. Only then did I hear it, the booming voice approaching like a rolling clap of thunder, the thudding footsteps the measured tread of doom. The giant laugh that made me tense. Not that loud people usually got to me. But because Willow's whole body seemed to shrivel, her expression settling into a tight mask that looked nothing like the young woman I'd just come to like and respect. "Forgive him," she said to me then as the door banged open with enough force to rattle the windows and a giant figure in jeans and a sport coat strode into my foyer like he owned the world.

CHAPTER SEVEN

S KIP ANDERSON LOOMED LARGER than life, no surprise there, the massive football player towering over all of us with his dark brown crewcut and fashionable five o'clock shadow, deep brown eyes scanning the interior before locking on his wife. Willow smiled at her husband though she didn't speak. Not that she didn't want to, maybe, but he never gave her the chance.

"This the joint?" So much for Olivia's nostalgia quote for the masses. Sounded like Skip never heard of Petunia's. And while Willow's dulcet tones soothed and enraptured, his rough and hearty words instantly grated. He tossed a large, leather duffle bag at Julian who caught it with a giant scowl before dropping it to the carpet with a disgusted look on his face. "Deal with my bag, Jeeves."

The manager's face tightened, Willow's hand rising ever so slightly to silence him while Skip leered at me.

"It'll do, I guess," he winked as if that was endearing. "God, this whole town has really gone downhill since we left, Wills. Why are we here again?"

Olivia's smile of greeting had frosted over at the corners but she wasn't going to let his attitude ruin anything. "Welcome home, Skip," she said. "We're so happy you're here after all the kind things you've said about Reading and all your help in ensuring our town prospers."

Weird, hadn't Jill said Olivia and Crew had gone to the airport to pick them up?

"Of course you are," he boomed. "But I'm only here for Wills." He looked around, clearly unimpressed. "No gym? No pool? Where's the bar?" Again his eyes settled on me. "You work here? Go get me a beer like a good girl."

Charming. But I'd handled puffed up arrogance more than enough in my life in New York and someone as overblown as Skip? Not my problem.

"Get your own beer," I said with a smile. "Corner store is a half a block. I'm sure you remember. If not, well. Can't miss it."

Olivia gasped at me, Willow's lips twitching. Even Julian looked shocked. And, for a second, I held still waiting to see what Skip's reaction to sass would be. Some guys like him? Temper, temper. Blew their crap all over the place. Others, yeah.

Skip fell into the "others" category.

Instead of going dark red in the face and exploding his arrogance all over the foyer like a spoiled little kid, he guffawed. A real, honest to god, I kid you not guffaw with knee slapping and snorting and a bit of hehaw in there for good measure. Willow winked slowly at me while her husband recovered.

"I like her!" He exhaled gustily. "Not much else about this craphole town to like, I seem to recall. But I do like *her*." He took one stride across the carpet on his big cowboy boots before hooking a massive arm around my shoulders and tucking me against his side. Where Carter's scent had a lusciousness to it I could lap up like a kitten with fresh milk, Skip's cologne almost suffocated me, the rigid power of his muscles like being tossed against a boulder. "Wills, can we keep her?"

Willow sighed softly, indulgently, but the apology in her eyes was aimed at me. "Let's get our rooms sorted out, Skip," she said. "We're running out of time if we want to stay on schedule."

Why wasn't I surprised she was the responsible one? Skip released me so suddenly I staggered a little. Now, don't get me wrong. I'm a pretty solid girl, 5'7" and athletic, thanks. But I'd never been hugged by a mountain before. The experience left me breathless and shaken. I couldn't imagine facing off against him on the field. Or how delicate Willow survived his attention.

"That's right," Olivia said, interjecting quickly before Skip could argue, his big face, nose broken sometime in the past at least once, darkening at last as his heavy brows pulled together. "We've lost a lot of time thanks to the accommodation issues."

"I make my own time," Skip grumbled, but he didn't seem like he was going to fight too hard. The mercurial switch in mood made me a bit nervous and I'm not ashamed to say when Willow held out her hand to encourage him to leave with her, I was happy to see him go.

"An hour, Olivia?" Willow waved to me while Daisy trotted down the stairs, beaming eagerly. The starlet followed my best friend as she retreated again, her grumbling and now irritated looking husband following behind her like some kind of unhappy watch dog.

The second they were out of sight I exhaled, only then realizing I'd held my breath since Skip's temper switch. Petunia whimpered softly and stared up at me as if she'd sensed his volatility too. Just confirming what I already decided.

Willow Pink? Awesome. Skip Anderson? Psycho in the making.

"You have a plan for the media, I take it?" Julian glared at Olivia while three people I hadn't even noticed waited by the front door for the mayor to answer. Skip's entry had utterly blocked their appearance, or I'd been so distracted by his overwhelming presence I'd somehow missed their arrival. But it was clear from the way they waited for Olivia to speak they were here with either Skip or Willow.

"We're taking care of that," Carter spoke up. I jumped a little, remembering he was still behind me. "I'm coordinating with the local police."

Julian grunted something that didn't sound supportive. "I'll be in my room," he said to no one in particular before sweeping up the staircase, leaving Skip's bag on the floor.

A tall, burly man well past his fifties with the look of an aging athlete to him crossed to the bag and hefted it in his hand. He smiled and nodded to me before holding out one hand.

"You probably don't remember me, Fiona," he said. "Matt Almeda." I shook with him, firm grasp meeting firm grasp. "Skip's coach."

Weird how he brought his coach with him...? "Wait, you were the football coach at the high school when I was there, weren't you?"

Matt shrugged, looking up the stairs. "Skip took me with him when he went to the pros." Ah, so that was a thing? "I'll check in on them. Thanks for taking us in like this. Not surprised with a mom like yours to raise you right." He'd have worked for my mother when she was principal at Reading High. "And your grandmother was a great lady. Nice to see Petunia's still here and running."

At least he maintained his common courtesy after leaving Reading. "Let me know if you need anything."

"Well, I need something." The woman with the gray pixie cut scowled at me. In fact, she'd been scowling pretty much the whole time she stood at my front door with her arms crossed over her chest. "My equipment." She gestured at the sitting room, now empty. "Where is it? I can't direct this stupid commercial without my equipment." Wow, she didn't have to match me for crab. Daisy would have her hands full with this one.

"I'll show you, Ms. Prichard," Carter said, nodding to me. "We set you up in one of the rooms."

She didn't bother to shake my hand, whoever she was. Not that I offered either. Pretty telling, the personalities Willow and Skip surrounded themselves with. And yet, an odd mix so far.

The final member of their little posse was on the phone, one of those headset things that sat in her ear and looked like it belonged in a science fiction movie. Her beige suit and white blouse made her overly bleached hair look yellow, but who was I to judge her? Except when her crisp, amber eyes met mine, the deep lines of stress and time in the business showing on her sallow complexion like she'd been forged in the fires of Hollywood and came out stronger for it.

"I still haven't seen a script, Stella. I'm not approving anything for Skip until I see a script." She didn't sound angry or upset or irritated. More bored, actually, distracted.

The gray haired woman sighed with so much drama I almost laughed. "It's an ad for a crappy town in Vermont," Stella said. "What kind of script are you hoping for, Evelyn?" She spun on the suited woman while Olivia's olive skin turned a dark shade of crimson. But the two women faced off as if they had no idea—or care—we were there. "Your precious footballer might think he's the important one here, but I can tell you Willow will feature. All he has to do is smile. That won't strain his dumb jock brain too much, you think?"

Evelyn's craggy face tightened. When she spoke, her lips puckered, deep lines forming around them, sign of a life-long smoker. "You might think you're someone in Hollywood, Stella Prichard. But you're directing a commercial for that same crappy Vermont town, not a feature, in case you missed it. My how far the mighty have fallen."

"I'm *directing*," Stella snarled, taking a step closer to Evelyn until they were toe-to-toe right in front of me, two massive egos butting heads, "as a *favor* for Willow."

"Face it, you're washed up," Evelyn said in that sickly sweet tone that cut deep.

"At least I'm not the agent for a failing football hero who's lost his edge," Stella shot back.

I'm positive it would have come to blows. So sure I was already in motion, if mentally, my body leaning toward them to break things up before one of them pulled the literal claws out and took a swing. The fact Olivia hadn't interjected made me wonder if she was hoping these two would take each other out and save her the agony.

But it was Julian who broke up the fight, appearing on the staircase with a grunt.

"Honestly, you two," he said, dripping disdain and all kinds of judgment. "Grow the hell up already."

Stella shot him a furious look but I felt the tension between the women break as they shifted their attention to Willow's manager.

"Mind your own business, Julian," Evelyn snapped.

"Considering I'm the only one in this little trio who actually has a viable career," he said, "you two can just shut up or get out. You're not ruining this weekend or this project for my Willow." He didn't change tone or position or even really seem to do anything special. But when he spoke again, I felt the chill of his tone go through me like a knife. "Understood?"

The women grumbled but the fight was over. At least, for now.

CHAPTER EIGHT

MOM APPEARED ABOUT FIVE minutes after I called her. A call I place two seconds after I found Mary and Betty Jones had left me—abandoned me—only to phone and tell me so in no uncertain terms.

"Not going to happen," Mary grunted at me after delivering her initial "We're so out of there for the duration of the festivities" message and I babbled something along the lines of please don't abandon me at a time like this. Not my proudest moment.

Instead, she informed me in no uncertain terms they would be keeping their distance until Willow and Skip and all the craziness that went with them was gone from Petunia's. I gaped at the handset as

Mary firmly turned me down no matter how much I begged, the sound of the TV blaring in the back ground. I could see the both of them in my mind's eye. Pictured them with their feet up on the coffee table, settling in with grins on their ungrateful faces. At least they went home and didn't decide to take over my apartment downstairs or the carriage house. All I'd need would be Petunia hopping up between them and hunkering down to a snack of offered potato chips I'd get to regret later in bed while she farted me a BBQ flavored symphony. "Olivia Walker can take her plans and stuff them."

"I'm not asking for Olivia," I said, hating the wheedling tone in my voice, going for guilt this time. "They won't be any more bother than any other guests."

Olivia had to choose that exact second to hurtle herself down the stairs and into my private apartment. To stare at me clutching the phone with a wild and harried look on her face before grasping me in her two strong hands and shaking me just enough to make my teeth rattle.

"Don't leave me alone up there," she begged with her words and her eyes and the firm and painful grasp of her fingers digging into my flesh. "Fee, please. Do something."

Mary laughed out loud and hung up in my ear. I knew then exactly how Olivia was feeling and, swallowing my pride, I did the only thing I could. I asked Lucy Fleming, that most amazing of moms, to come to my rescue. And when the front door breezed open, my lovely mother entering as if she were coming to a ball, a bit overdressed in a nice suit and with her hair and makeup pristine as if she expected my call to come in, I was shocked to find my still jean and button upped favoring father had tagged along behind her.

Wouldn't you know the irritating man who used to be sheriff and was now retired grinned as if he couldn't wait to see this all turn into a massive disaster?

Olivia leaped on Mom the second she appeared, hugging her in vague desperation. Ever since the murder of Mason Patterson on Valentine's Day and my mother's firm and collected offer of support, Olivia had mostly avoided Mom. Whether out of nervousness she might want the mayor's job herself or just embarrassment we'd sampled that side of her I didn't know. But seeing Olivia's reaction now made me grin behind one hand and clear my throat so I didn't giggle.

"How exciting, sweetie," Mom said, extracting herself from Olivia and coming to hug me before offering Petunia a loving scratch on her ear. The pug's happy groan of contentment filled the foyer. "Are they really here? Now?"

"Upstairs." I nodded. "Betty and Mary—"

"Now, don't you worry a bit," Mom said, beaming. Like she hadn't been dying since my grandmother passed away to get her hands on Petunia's kitchen. Mom's culinary skills were the envy of my tummy and I felt a whole lot better, not just thanks to her comforting presence. We wouldn't starve and I wouldn't poison anyone with my cooking. Things were looking up. "John and I are happy to help, aren't we, John?"

Dad winked at me before his old gruffness returned, the façade of his bluster making me shake my head. "I had plans for today," he said.

Yeah. Right.

Olivia beamed at both of them as if she hadn't been here the whole time and missed the subtleties of what just happened. "This is perfect," she said. "I'm off to check on the parade. Don't let anyone in who's not on the list." She hurried toward the front door while we watched her go. It wasn't until the door slammed shut behind her—the next person that slammed my door was going to get a very firm talking to that involved physical violence and maybe an escort to the E.R.—Dad turned back with a frown and open hands.

"List?"

I laughed then, shrugged. "Someone has a list, Dad. Somewhere. I'm sure of it."

Neither of my parents answered, interrupted by the swing of the kitchen door as Mr. and Mrs. Johansen clattered out into the foyer, the sound of their rollie wheels on tile turning to muffled thuds as they crossed to the carpet and paused next to me.

"I'm so sorry, dear," Shirley Johansen said while she peeked up the stairs with cheeks pinking. "I suppose we'll have to be moving on."

Olivia had asked for this, but no way was I going to kick out my guests. "I'm sorry to hear that," I said. "You're more than welcome to stay."

Her husband, Dick, seemed less curious about my other guests than he did annoyed. "A bit of warning would have been nice," he huffed.

"Tell me about it." I turned to the sideboard and my computer, checking them out as I did. "I wasn't given a choice. I'm so sorry this happened. If you decide to return to Reading anytime soon, please accept a night on me for your trouble." The printer chugged off a receipt and I handed it over.

Shirley patted her husband's arm with one hand. "I would have loved to stay," she said. "Maybe go looking for the treasure hoard everyone is talking about."

"Not with weird people lurking and peeking in windows! Damned paparazzi or whatever you call them." Dick scowled at me. "Next time we're in Reading we're staying at the lodge."

I watched them go, my own frown forming. I turned away from my parents and glared at the kitchen door, mind whirling even as I headed for the garden with murder on my mind. Bad enough Pamela had snuck in. Were there reporters taking pictures in my yard even now?

Mom and Dad followed, Petunia on my heels. The four of us exited the kitchen door, the normally tall plants of the English style garden just beginning to bud. While I usually had to cross to the center of the double sized lot and the koi pond to spot the carriage house's full outline, without foliage in the way it was easy enough to see. And to catch the figure standing at the corner of the building, looking in a window.

Dad's hand fell on my shoulder and held me back while I huffed in fury at the intrusion.

"Let me handle it," he said. But before he could act—or I could helpfully shout at him to arrest the intruder even though that wasn't his job anymore—the figure dodged toward the fence that divided my property from the Munroe house next door and disappeared.

"It's a shame," Mom said, "but it's bound to happen, Fee."

I grunted at the departing figure. "I'll have to tell Crew," I said. "I won't have Petunia's overrun with reporters."

Dad turned me around and guided me into the kitchen, enough sympathy on his face I believed he wasn't teasing me.

"Do Willow and Skip have security?" He sounded like his old law enforcement self.

"They do," I said. And wondered where Carter had gotten himself off to. Right, he mentioned something about the sheriff, hadn't he? "I think he's coordinating with Crew." When I needed them here, damn it. Typical.

CHAPTER NINE

I WASN'T EXPECTING THE kitchen door to swing open and for Olivia to return in a bustle. Nor for her impatient finger snap that was meant, I suppose, to make us jump to attention.

"Change in plans," she snarled. "The media are coming now. We need to get on the parade yesterday. Go change, Fiona. You're up."

Wait, what? "Huh?" So intelligent, this internal and then external conversation. But I was stunned and stumped, thank you. Best I could muster in the face of what the actual…?

"As host to our guests, you're in the parade," she said like this had already been decided and I was just being troublesome to give her an ulcer. "Go. Change.

Now." And then she was gone, the door swinging slowly shut behind her.

It took Daisy to guide me downstairs, to pick out an outfit for me and do my hair into a reasonable facsimile of an upsweep. To apply makeup and lipstick while I softly protested, stunned all over again but now out of sheer terror. The parade? Why was I in the parade? I didn't even like standing on a stage and handing things to people. Public displays made me nauseated. And Olivia wanted me to wave and smile at all of Reading?

"You'll be fabulous," Daisy gushed as she helped me into a soft gold sweater I'd been saving for a possible date with Crew Turner or some other male personage if I ever had the chance to date again without becoming an old, withered woman with no social life. Hey, wait a minute... She fussed over my black dress pants and high heels, because black was the new black, I guess. Not exactly showgirl material, but at least I didn't look like I plunged toilets for a living. "Just sit and wave and pretend you're the queen of Reading." She beamed as she showed me, nodding and smiling and curving her hand at the imaginary crowd.

"If it's so great," I muttered while she shoved me up the stairs and into the foyer, past my evilly grinning father, my pug panting at my feet with more enthusiasm than she should have been showing at a time like this, "why don't you do it?"

"Because," Daisy said, leading me past Mom who clasped her hands under her chin and smiled in delight at my transformation just the worst betrayal I could ever imagine. Why wasn't she rescuing me from this massive mistake? "I'm not Fiona Fleming."

The bright sunlight caught my eyes, and I blinked into it like a grumpy grizzly emerging from a long winter's sleep. If it weren't for Daisy I would have tumbled down the stairs in the ridiculous heels she'd put me in—why did I own these monstrosities again?—and embarrassed myself and Reading by landing on my face.

Instead, she held my elbow in a firmly practiced grip, walking me down to the street and—get this— the large and elaborately painted horse-drawn wagon waiting for me.

Petunia tolerated Carter's assistance when he appeared at her side to boost her into the dark green velvet seat, before turning to offer me his hand. Daisy backed off, though I wasn't paying attention to her at the moment. Not with those eyes locked on mine and that smile and the way his hand felt when I took it in mine. Before I knew it I was sitting beside my pug, with my back to the two Clydesdales and the driver, wondering what the hell just happened and had I lost my mind somewhere since this morning...?

Didn't help I spotted Crew Turner across the street talking with Robert and Jill. Or that he raised his eyebrows at me before waving. I waved back, not knowing what else to do, Daisy's ridiculous queenly curve all I could muster. I looked like an idiot.

"Hey, Fee." The driver glanced over his shoulder, grinned at me. Took me a second, but I smiled back at the young man.

"Hi, Hank," I said, releasing some of the tension and finding the ability to speak again. "How's the ponies?" He and his father ran the local stable, though from what I'd heard they'd been struggling since the equestrian center got underway again. I hoped the developer, Jared Wilkins, would be willing to work with them, but it wasn't up to me.

"They're just happy it's spring," he laughed, lines crinkling around the edges of his brown eyes. Boyish good looks fading in his late twenties, he needed a haircut and a shave, but I figured the horses didn't care what he looked like. "You okay? You seem a bit pale."

"Just going with Olivia's little flow for today," I said as the door to Petunia's opened again and the mayor swept out with Willow, Skip and entourage in tow. "Tell me why we're doing this again?"

Hank laughed. "For the good of Reading," he said, voice low and with a grin before turning away while Olivia arrived with her very special guests.

"Ah, Fiona," she said as if she wasn't expecting me. "Skip, I hope you're all right with sharing with your host while I steal away with your lovely wife?"

Oh, *come on.* Seriously? Only then did I look up and notice the second wagon behind us, Hank's dad, Hank Sr., with his hands on the reins and a grumpy look on his lined face.

Skip seemed out of it a moment, wavering slightly. Dear god, was he drunk? He leaned in to Willow who flinched away before spinning and marching to the other wagon. Skip glared after her, face darkening before he looked back to Olivia.

"Whatever," he growled, slurring slightly. "Just get this stupid whatever you call it over with."

This was going to be delightful, wasn't it? I hugged Petunia to my hip, jaw clenching, as Skip tried to climb into the wagon on his own. He slipped the first time, swearing, hands catching at the entry to the carriage, rocking the whole thing violently. I heard Hank curse himself, the horses stomping in protest, bells on their harness jingling. Carter tucked in behind the football player and subtly boosted him, allowing Skip to finally make it up and into the wagon, landing heavily on the seat across from me.

I peeked around his massive bulk, saw that Olivia was scated with Willow already, looking all cozy and not grumpy and stoned or boozed out or whatever Skip was. Maybe both.

My companion, meanwhile, reached into the pocket of his sport coat, taking three tries to retrieve the flask before opening it with shaking fingers and upending it into his mouth. Yup, still could be both. Mixing drugs and alcohol could get him this wasted in the short time it took for the parade to assemble. As if as an afterthought he looked at me, bleary and unfocused, before offering his flask to me.

I was so out of here. But the second I moved to stand, to run and hide like the Jones sisters, to leave this pathetic, overblown idiot to make a fool of himself alone, I heard it. The plaintive cries of the self-proclaimed Queen of the Bakery. And my butt cheeks clenched so hard I couldn't move.

Vivian French, my old rival from high school who'd made it her mission since I came home to Reading to make sure I knew nothing had changed, stood next to Olivia's carriage. Dressed in white fur from head to toe. *Fur.* As if she were some kind of magical snow angel or Wicked Witch of the Nauseating or something equally ridiculous.

"You said," her plaintive cry reached me and warmed the cold, bitter cockles of my heart. "You *promised.*"

"That's what the convertible in the back is for," Olivia said, big, fake smile plastered all over her face. "You're lucky to be in the parade at all, Vivian. Get in line or don't come. I don't are. We're leaving. Now."

Vivian huffed and puffed and looked up. Forward. To the carriage and Skip and over that football star's shoulder and into my green, watching eyes. Saw me smile, wave as Daisy taught me, this time meaning every single moment of it to the core of my horrible, vengeful being. And turned as pale as the fur she wore.

For that reason and that reason only I stayed on the green velvet seat across from the horrible man I was learning to despise and settled in to grit my teeth and do my part for the good of Reading.

CHAPTER TEN

"That's right! You know you love me!"

It wasn't even ten minutes later and I'd have happily traded places with Vivian and her dumb outfit. Or better yet, biffed Skip Anderson over the side and run for the hills if I thought I could get away with it. The moment the carriage began to move, Hank clucking softly to the team, Skip's abrasive running commentary started up and didn't stop. If anything, the slur in his voice grew worse, not better, until he was barely coherent and immensely loud.

He'd stood for his latest tirade, in line with the towering statue of Captain Reading, perhaps triggered by the sight of the jauntily cocky privateer's grim grin. I lived in fear of Skip collapsing on top of me and Petunia and pinning us to the green velvet as he swayed with the roll of the carriage over the street.

"He needs to sit down," Hank hissed over his shoulder at me.

"So you tell him," I shot back, hugging my pug to me for dear life.

Skip did us all a solid and crashed to the bench, belching a massive wave of flammable gas over me, saluting the statue with narrowed eyes before grinning like this whole situation was a personal joke. "'Scuse," he said into one fist.

Any plans I had to follow Daisy's advice to wave and smile were long gone. Instead, I got to enjoy the humiliation of having every single resident of Reading—lining the streets for a look at their favorite stars—stare in shock and horror as Skip Anderson proceeded to lean over the edge of the carriage and noisily empty his stomach down the side of the pretty paintjob.

How could one person have so much food inside them? And why was the bulk of it still identifiable? I'd never eat a hamburger again for as long as I lived.

"I'm billing Olivia for that," Hank muttered.

Loyalty to Reading aside? I couldn't wait to talk to Pamela and have her write the story of a lifetime.

The press were having a field day, obviously, from the not so subtle ways they crowded as best they could despite the efforts of the Curtis County sheriff's department. Jill, Crew and Robert had their hands full, the media and even the watching crowd pressing against the barricades while Carter and a few others in dark suits cruised like watchful panthers with sunglasses and earbuds, looking dangerous enough to hold the bulk of the curious back from the carriages. Didn't keep the giant lenses from pointing at us, a few smirks in the gathering. One man in particular, small and compact, caught my attention because he was the bravest of the bunch, making it all the way to the street before Jill could chase him back. He grinned at me, waved in jaunty greeting, dark curls a deeper red than mine and with that saucy look brash men get when they're having fun before disappearing into the crowd again.

Skip noticed, lurching to his feet, screaming after him. "RUSSELL! You little weasel, I'll..." The rest was a garbled mess of words that made no sense while Skip's energy finally seemed to fade and he sat once more, mumbling into his flask.

Please, *please*. I just needed this to be over. And for Petunia and I to exit without getting crushed by a football player in a stupor.

Town hall appeared at the end of the street, the podium we'd been heading for finally in view. While Reading was a small place, this whole parade joke and a half had lasted far longer than it should have been permitted to. Once Skip was out of the carriage I was hoofing it back to Petunia's, even if I had to go in my bare feet and carry these stupid shoes in one hand and the portly pug in the other.

Another minute. That was all I needed. I started counting down from sixty to one, tracking the seconds by my heartbeats that were a bit too fast for regular time but kept losing my place. And Skip wasn't going to give me the reprieve I needed. Of course not. As Hank pulled the Clydes to a halt next to the podium, the drunk—and possibly stoned, I voted for both because surely there was layers to his intoxication I had yet to fathom—football star once more rose to stand over me, towering above the crowd who'd followed from the parade route. He swayed as he did, staring down over those who gazed up at him, some even with a bit of respect remaining.

Until he opened his damned fool mouth.

"This town," he shouted, "is the worst piece of crap garbage heap town ever. Reading sucks!" Everyone stared in shock, me included, while Willow hung her head, hand over her face, and Olivia bolted out the side of her carriage, running toward us. Too late. A few expletives escaped him before his coherence returned. "I hate this place. I've always hated it. You're all pathetic for staying. As stupid as believing any of you could ever amount to anything or anyone." Wait, was he talking about them? Or himself? Wow, this was a show I really wished I'd missed. Where was my quiet garden afternoon when I needed it? Instead of getting to gape at the story Jill would have told me later, nicely distanced from and suitably horrified and amused by her experience and his idiocy, I was living it firsthand.

Lucky me.

Skip swayed on his feet, tossing back the last of the liquid in his flask. "I hope you rot here forever."

The booing started at the back of the crowd but built up volume and layers pretty quickly. Olivia's dash ended abruptly as Carter stopped her, frowning at her, leaning in to say something. Likely to prevent her from attacking the man he worked for. I know if

I was her I'd be ready to kill him and hide the body and never, ever speak of this again.

Oddly funny, though, come to think of it. Enough so I felt a hysterical giggle building in the back of my throat, the kind of amusement that would end in me unable to breathe with tears pouring down my face and making a massive fool of myself because this wasn't funny. Not really. Though in the wake of Skip's little show, me breaking down into bits and pieces would hardly be noticed, so there was that saving grace to keep me from utter humiliation.

I failed to notice, in my distraction with my own struggles, that Skip had fallen suddenly silent. It wasn't until the crowd went quiet I looked up, while the shadow of the mountain that was the football player leaned into the shade of the real mountain backdrop. Wait, why did it feel like he was coming toward me?

It wasn't until he landed on me, sagging into my lap, I realized my original terrified concern had come true. Only, this wasn't some ordinary collapse, not a drug or alcohol unconsciousness, a tumble into sleep or passing out from mere chemical conditioning. No, his fall was made worse when I tried to push him off and felt that instant—that impossible to miss moment of utter horror—when he breathed his last acerbic breath into the spring air.

In the stunning sunshine, dressed in the sweater I'd wanted to share with someone who could treat me like I meant something to them, I half-shrank, half-sagged under the dead body of Reading's most famous son.

CHAPTER ELEVEN

WHILE I WAS ACCUSTOMED to dead bodies by now, having one laying across my lap for any length of time had a vastly different feel to, say, finding one drowned in my koi pond or observing from a distance as one collapsed into a dosed slice of chocolate cake. Up close and personal? Not exactly my favorite.

I know there was screaming (likely my own) and shouting (from all around me) and panic (combination of the two), but the time it took for Skip Anderson to gasp his last and someone to manhandle the bulky body from my person seemed far longer than absolutely necessary. Mind you, I would have preferred not to be part of the process at all, thanks very much, but in retrospect I suppose a few seconds with the freshly dead corpse wasn't that big a deal.

Reality, however? I'm positive it took Crew Turner six million years to do the deed. At least it felt that long, time stretched out into infinity tainted by the reek of alcohol, the radiating residue of the dead body's ambient heat, the overpowering stench of his cologne and some bodily fluids that had to have escaped upon his passing. All while I was being slowly and permanently damaged by the event in question.

Yes, I know. The previous comes across as rather clinical and detached. Would you prefer I confessed that the second Skip's body hit the deck and my person I started shrieking like a banshee, backpedaling with my high heels scraping over the floor of the carriage while he slowly slithered down to wedge into the small space between the seats, big head draped over my thigh, blackness closing in while I struggled to breathe past my endless, throat tearing screams?

There you go, then. You're welcome.

I felt the carriage rock, heard someone grunt. Where was Hank, damn it? My attempts to shove

Skip off me only succeeded in pushing him further and deeper into the space between the benches, trapping me utterly beneath dead weight and green velvet. All the sensation in my legs had left, squashed out by the weight of him, cutting off circulation to my lower extremities. Would I have to have them amputated? Was he not only scarring my psyche but this disaster on the path to rendering me a double amputee? Anything was preferable to sitting there, staring down at the corpse that used me for a resting place. I would have happily sawed off my own legs just to escape.

"Fee, breathe." And then Crew was there, face tight and drawn, voice so low, so deep it penetrated my screaming and cut off the sound. My ears rang from my own vocal protest and I finally managed a full, shaking breath, seeing him waver over me and knew as warm wetness trickled down my cheeks I was crying. And that Crew Turner witnessed it.

That was a big slap to the face, enough to pull me together and shake off the shock of my predicament. I doubted anyone could fault me my initial reaction, but I was a Fleming, damn it. I didn't cry in public—not even when I found out my ex-boyfriend of five years had been making a fool of me by cheating our entire relationship. Not when I left Reading for what I thought was forever. Not when my Grandmother Iris died. I didn't cry. Especially not in front of someone like him.

Crew's big hands grasped Skip, firmly and efficiently pulling him off me and back toward the other bench. It took every single scrap of control I had in my body not to scramble out the rest of the way and run home, still screaming, and into the nearest hot shower, clothes or no clothes. Instead, I kept my eyes fixed on Crew and let him do his job while I went for zen.

Breathe in. Breathe out.

Jill appeared over my right shoulder, the carriage rocking as she stepped up on the wheel well and settled one hand on my arm. That touch meant more to me than she would ever know and I blinked away the last of my terror driven tears, wiping my face with both hands, looking down at the fawn pug beside me who stared at Crew as if she, too, was overwhelmed by what just happened. I hugged her to me, checking her over, using that focus as the means to ignore what Crew was doing. How his quick examination of the body did nothing to free me, my calves and feet still tangled up with the corpse.

"Looks like an OD," Crew muttered, clearly for Jill but reaching me, too.

"He was drinking from a flask and seemed either drunk or stoned when he got in at Petunia's." Hey, that was more like it. Good one, Fee. Big girl panties were a bit snug but they offered awesome support.

"Fee," Crew leaned toward me, one hand on my thigh, his touch layering over the steady presence of Jill's. I wasn't alone. It was okay. And it was just a dead guy. No biggie or anything. Breathe in. "Are you all right?" Breathe out.

I nodded, swallowed, tried a smile while my cheeks twitched and my lips trembled. "Just get us out of this, okay?" Yes, I thought of Petunia. Of course I did. I wasn't that far gone. Yet.

"Can you give me one more minute?" He winced a little, glanced at Jill. "Dr. Aberstock is right here and I want him to look before I move you."

Evidence preservation. Right. I had to think like a cop at a time like this, even if I never got to be one. "Just tell him to hurry up," I said between clenched teeth. Petunia shivered next to me, whining softly while Crew retreated and was replaced by the elderly and mild mannered Dr. Aberstock. He patted my hand before taking a look at Skip while I stared at

Petunia's wrinkled noggin and ignored the loud chatter of the crowd, the way the wind had turned chill and the fact the sun had gone behind a cloud at some point and now I wished I had a winter coat.

I knew it was shock, that a stiff shot of something with alcohol in it and a block of time to process was what I really needed. Instead, I got to sit there and listen to Dr. Aberstock hum softly to himself while his kindly grandfather persona showed nothing of the care he took in his work before speaking, presumably to Crew.

"Signs of overdose." He didn't sound surprised. "I'll have to do a full tox panel, though, so don't quote me. But it certainly looks that way."

"Thanks, Doc." I felt Dr. Aberstock leave, looked up when Crew reappeared. "I just need to look you over, is that all right?" How careful he sounded, how slow and gentle. Like I'd break if he wasn't soft and cautious. Well, maybe he was right. I'd never seen him look so worried before. What expression had my face twisted into that he seemed so afraid of my present state of mind?

"It's fine," I said. Nodded and exhaled through my open mouth. Unclenched my hands from around Petunia. Inhaled. "I'm fine."

"I know you are," Crew said. "I'll be fast." He scanned me with his gaze, my legs, my lap. Looked at my fingers, the floor under my feet. "Did he touch you besides falling on you? At any point?"

I shook my head, feeling Daisy's careful upsweep come loose, the massive weight of my red hair tumbling around me. "Just when he fell," I said. "But he did puke over the side at one point. In front of Sammy's Coffee." And Captain Reading's statue.

"I've got it here, boss," Jill said. "I'll bag some for Doc."

Crew's big hand rose, held out toward me. "Good enough for me. Come on, Fee. Let's get you out of here."

I wasn't even sure I could stand, that my wobbly legs would support me. It took Crew and Jill, who leaned in over the edge of the carriage, to untangle me the rest of the way from Skip, his long legs taking up way too much space as far as I was concerned. I didn't look up, couldn't, kept my eyes locked on the toes of my high heels. Stumbled with Petunia in my grasp and almost fell until strong arms caught me and swung me up and out of the way.

So tempting to lay my head on Crew's shoulder, to breathe in the scent of his fabric softener—the same one we used at Petunia's—and wash away the stench of Skip, to clutch at the collar of the sheriff's uniform shirt and cry into the faint shadow of his beard. I think I would have, too. Just given in to the horrible event I'd endured, if it weren't for Robert.

"Poor Fanny," my cousin said, smirk as nasty as I'd ever seen it. "Need a big strong man to take care of you, little girl?"

The thing was I didn't get to chew his head off. Was instantly prepared to, almost thanked him for knocking me back into anger and irritation and out of this odd weakness I felt. But someone beat me to it.

"Officer Carlisle," Crew's rumbling voice reached me through the walls of his chest, vibrating into my body from our close contact as he stood there on the sidewalk with me in his arms, my pug cuddled on top, "the next time you open your mouth, you'd better have something helpful to say or you'll be finding a new vocation."

Robert fish lipped even as Crew set me carefully down on the sidewalk and steadied me with both hands on my shoulders. I looked up at him, Petunia chuffing her soft concern, seeing odd things in his

I'd never been so happy to see Petunia's, the towering white colonial beckoning me to hurry inside and slam the door—yes, slam it as hard as I could—and go hide somewhere with a bottle of wine or maybe some scotch. Instead, I ran up the stairs, depositing my pug into the foyer, and hugged my best friend who hurtled herself into my arms.

"Fee." Daisy whispered my name before letting me go. "Willow's upstairs. She's locked herself in her room and won't let anyone in." She bit her full lower lip, glancing first at Mom then Dad. "This is a disaster."

"You're telling me." Olivia stormed in behind us, pushing Mom out of the way, confronting me, red faced and trembling like this was somehow my fault. "What the hell just happened?"

I would have hit her. I'm positive my fist, clenched at my side, would have made impressive contact with her face. I even saw it play out in my head, the swing, the impact, the massive satisfaction just before the searing pain in my knuckles told me I'd made a terrible life choice. I had a temper, I'd never tried to deny that. But I wasn't the kind of person who usually resorted to physical violence,

face I wasn't in any kind of position to process just now.

"I'll have Jill escort you home," he said. "When you're ready."

"That's all right, Crew." And then Dad was there, Mom, my mother hugging me so tight Petunia squeaked in protest. "We'll take care of her."

I looked back over my shoulder, wobbling on my stupid shoes, at the sight of Crew barking orders, the crowd snapping photos, feeling like I was moving underwater and out of focus, and for once not even remotely curious about what happened.

I just wanted to go home.

CHAPTER TWELVE

I MADE IT A block and just outside the crush of onlookers when my legs gave out. Mom took Petunia, Dad supporting me but as soon as I was able to kick off the idiotic shoes on my sore and unhappy feet I felt a ton better.

"I'm okay, I promise," I said, now annoyed and grasping for that emotion as a source of strength. I shrugged Dad's arm off and crossed my own over my chest, hugging myself while I stomped toward Petunia's, the dirty pavement under my bare feet icy cold and disgusting but adding an extra layer to my anger. Perfect. Being mad would get me home without another dumb show of weakness and vulnerability.

Oh. My. *God*. Did I really let Crew he[ ] his arms like some kind of damsel in distress [ ] an action hero? In front of the entire damne[ ] Including, I now recalled, the white-furred s[ ] Bakery Queen who'd glared like she planne[ ] downfall?

Screw Vivian. But honestly. I'd never, ever [ ] this down. Didn't help I could still smell him on [ ] either. Or that my pillow had that same scent as [ ] constant reminder. Time to switch fabric softeners.

"It'll only be a matter of time before the press converges on the B&B." Dad's grim tone and long stride helped me focus. I had to hurry to keep up, poor Mom huffing to match our pace. I turned and took the pug from her, lightening her load before continuing on.

"I'll talk to Carter," I said. "But it's a pretty good bet the whole slew will be leaving Reading in short order. So the press can come at me all they want. There won't be anyone here to badger."

"Fee." Dad's tone sounded choked and when I looked up at him his anxiety was clear. "Skip died on you." He seemed to hesitate before rushing on. "You're the one they're going to want to talk to."

Oh, crap. And just freaking lovely.

despite the elementary school precedent that had left Vivian with a broken nose of her own.

What about this whole situation had turned me into a budding pugilist?

"Back off, Olivia." Mom had shown our mayor her teeth already, on Valentine's Day. And while my kindhearted and efficient mother had been a teacher and a principal for years, I'd only ever been personally guided by her steady and reasonable style of encouragement and punishment. To see her yet again lose her cool, show her own temper, well. It made me feel a bit better about my leanings toward punching the woman in the face.

"Our town is at stake here, Lucy," Olivia snapped back.

"Blaming Fiona for the death of Skip Anderson isn't doing you one scrap of good, though, is it?" Mom's return to level, insistent logic visibly diffused the mayor as she went on. "Clearly the young man suffered from some kind of physical issue."

That was a tactful way to put things when we all knew the truth of the situation.

"You mean he was a drug addict and an alcoholic," a voice interrupted while the director, Stella, thudded her way down the stairs, Evelyn and

Matt at her back, Julian huffing after them. "And likely died of an OD after downing a quart of whiskey and however many pills he needed to get through today."

Well, that was interesting information Crew needed. And look at me, going all curious and investigative and everything despite what happened. That turn of focus helped me feel better than anything else had.

"I've heard enough of you disparaging my client," Evelyn said, sounding like she might even mean it.

But Matt sighed as the four reached the foyer floor and shook his head. "Except, Evie, Stella is right and we've both been hiding it for a year now."

"Whatever." The director had her bags in her hands, face pinched in fury. "This has been nothing but a disaster from the instant I agreed to assist. No matter how much I adore Willow, I will not tolerate being tied to a scandal of this nature. Now, if you'll excuse me, I'm going home to L.A. and plan to forget any of this ever happened."

"No one is going anywhere." When had Crew arrived? I turned to find him silhouetted in the sunlight, standing in the doorway of Petunia's. He calmly and politely closed the door behind him without slamming it and my estimation of him skyrocketed. Might have had something to do with the fact I was still humming over being held in those arms, against that chest. The scent of him clinging to me with insistent strength. Or the shock.

Sure. Let's call it the shock.

"You can't hold us here." Stella's splutter covered something. But what? I was just too muddled up to figure it out.

That's what Crew was for, I guess. "Until we know for certain Skip's death was an accident, I'm going to need to ask all of you to stay here and wait for the coroner to do his job."

The protesting started immediately, from Matt and Evelyn, Stella's voice louder than the rest, while Julian crossed his arms over his chest and muttered under his breath. Even Olivia seemed unhappy with Crew's orders, hands clenched at her sides as she pushed past me and got in her own sheriff's face.

"You can't turn our guests into prisoners," she snarled, her words cutting through the rest and rendering them silent.

"Yes," Willow said, appearing at the top of the stairs, looking as fragile and wavering as I felt. "He can. And he should. I want answers as much as the sheriff does."

"Willow." Julian hurried up toward her though Carter stood behind her, concern on his handsome face. But her manager ignored the security guard, guiding his client down toward us when it was clear she wasn't going to just turn around on her own. "You really should be in your room resting. You've had a terrible shock."

"We all have," she said, voice clear despite her pale cheeks, the redness of her large eyes. When I cried, I got this horrible rash like red mottling on my face and neck, even down into my cleavage. Hideous legacy of a redhead. But Willow? She looked like a waif, an elvish princess who'd wept silver magic tears for her fallen lover just before breaking into ethereal song over the loss. Not jealous or anything. "Sheriff Turner, we're here to cooperate in any way you need. As long as Fiona is willing to continue to host us after what happened." She came to me, hesitant and clearly distressed, opening her arms. I hugged her, feeling again the frailness of her body but this time sensing the core of steel that kept her erect and moving forward despite her grief. Much stronger than I'd given her credit for. "Fee, I'm so sorry. How horrible for you."

"I'm sorry too," I whispered back, surprised to find how choked up I felt. "It must have been terrible, seeing it happen and not being able to do anything."

She blinked tears that wet her long, thick lashes, near translucent skin wet with them while they tracked from her eyes. "We didn't know what was going on. I thought Skip fell. He was so..." She looked away, embarrassment clear from the bright red spots that formed on the points of her cheekbones, her collarbones and the way her hands flexed into fists a moment. "He was drunk and the painkillers always made him so unsettled."

Confirmation then of what Stella was saying. I heard scratching, turned to find Crew writing her words down in his little book. He looked up and met my eyes, his eyebrows arched before he spoke, though his question was addressed to Willow.

"Was he taking a lot of medication, Ms. Pink?" Not a scrap of judgment in that voice. He was learning, then. The Crew I'd first met had a hard time putting those he questioned at ease. Or maybe that was just when he interrogated me.

"He suffered multiple concussions over the years," Matt spoke up for her. "Not to mention other injuries." He shrugged like it was no big deal. "The man played pro ball for a living. He was a gladiator. And that meant pain."

Crew grunted softly while Dad shifted beside me. I was well aware my father played football in high school and college and from the expression on Crew's face he had inside knowledge of the kind of hurt the coach was talking about.

"What was he taking?" Crew's pen paused.

"Vicodin, mostly," Matt said, suddenly sounding uncomfortable, head lowering, looking away from Willow.

"Mostly," she said. Breathlessly, as if unsurprised but horribly disappointed. "What else, Matt? What was he experimenting with this time?"

"It was the last concussion," his coach blurted. "You know it did a number on him."

"I'm well aware of that fact." How precise she sounded, almost offended. "What was he taking?"

"A new painkiller one of the team docs recommended." Matt seemed to sag, sad and broken. "He called it Quexol." Matt met my eyes. "But he stopped taking it because he said it made him feel off. So he was back on the Vicodin."

Crew's phone rang. The interruption as he took the call seemed to break the spell holding everyone in thrall to what was likely supposed to be a private conversation between Skip's coach and his wife. I grasped her hand gently in mine and she met my gaze with her own stunned and disillusioned hurt.

"Stay as long as you need," I said. "I'll make sure the house is yours."

"Thank you, Fee," she said. "For everything."

I felt her drifting, could only imagine her emotional and mental state. And held onto her hand as Crew hung up and, grim, cleared his throat.

"I take it that's bad news." Dad sounded so much like the sheriff—well, he'd been one enough years himself the tone never went away—I looked back and forth between them as Crew answered.

"How is this Quexol administered?" He directed that at Matt.

"Injection," the coach said automatically. "But, like I said, he stopped taking it. Hadn't had any in about a week. Left it home, or said he did."

"So the injection site and small fresh bruise on the back of his thigh," Crew said, "that Doc just found. No chance it's from him jabbing himself?"

Willow gasped softly and for a moment I pinged with anger toward the sheriff.

But it was Matt's grim head shake that shifted me from irritation at Crew's return to coarseness with questioning and to the chill of certainty this wasn't an accident. "No way. He hated the stuff. And he'd had so much of his regular dose today already if he had taken Quexol…"

He left that hanging. Because the rest was obvious.

"It would have killed him," Crew finished. "Which means you're all staying put. Until I figure out who murdered Skip Anderson."

CHAPTER THIRTEEN

THE KITCHEN SEEMED AN oasis, empty without Betty Jones puttering around preparing for afternoon tea. Good thing the whole town was still in an uproar. I'd have to turn people away from our new ritual, one that seemed to have generated a great deal of enthusiastic support from locals since we started it last year.

I stared out the kitchen windows into the backyard, trying to pull myself together and failing miserably. My mind kept drifting back to being in the carriage, the towering form of Skip falling in slow, mountainous motion on top of me. Chances are I'd be in for some lovely nightmares the next little while—if not the rest of my freaking life. Good thing

I had Petunia to hug at night when the terrors came to roost.

Speaking of my pug, I looked down to find her sitting on my cold and still bare toes, her big brown eyes gazing at me with the kind of vapid happiness that endeared her to everyone she met. She snorted softly when she realized I was paying attention to her at last, tongue lolling out while she shifted her position, the whites showing around her bulging gaze.

"Hungry, sweet girl?" Feeding her would give me something to do for two seconds and distract me from the endless cycle of the memory of Skip's death. A banana didn't take long to peel or smear with peanut butter and I sat on the stool with the drooling dog at my feet and fed her one portion at a time while she grumbled at me to go faster, cinnamon bun tail wiggling in ridiculously adorable enthusiasm. "He didn't hurt you, did he, baby?" I had found myself talking to her a lot since I moved back home, Petunia often my only source of interaction once night fell. It had become an easy kind of thing to do, a one-sided conversation that she seemed to enjoy and certainly didn't begrudge. So that made me a bit nuts and probably doomed me to a life alone like my grandmother with a long line of Petunia's into infinity to fart and snuggle and grunt in response to my conversations.

I could think of harder lives to live.

She didn't seem any worse for wear, recovered from her own shocked state and back to Petunia happy. I wiped my fingers on the tea towel next to the counter while she devoured the last slice of nutty banana goodness, considering running her to the vet just in case. And squeaked in surprise as someone moved outside the kitchen door, jerking me from my solemn pet mom thoughts.

Pamela again, damn her for scaring me like that. I waved her inside and she joined me, hugging me awkwardly like that was what you did between friends when one just bore the brunt of a murder victim's body. To top off the uncomfortable closeness, she released me then patted my shoulder as if I were Petunia.

"You're okay?" As weird as that whole encounter was, her concern was genuine, I could feel that and forgave what came before as her making an effort that actually touched me deeply. "We were worried. Aundrea and Jared were at the podium and watched the whole thing. They said you were hurt." Nice to know she actually cared, that they all did, after what we'd been through together. While it could have gone the other way after the death of Pete Wilkins and Mason Patterson, I took it as a gift I had found friends in this town despite the way I left and did my best not to let the rise of burning in the back of my throat turn into sobs.

"I wasn't hurt," I said. "I'm fine." Yup, and saying that word over and over again was going to make being "fine" real. Sure was.

Pamela sighed, shook her head. "It's a terrible tragedy," she said.

"You want to know what happened." Not a question. I felt tired suddenly, the adrenaline and the shock finally wearing off until I felt like a noodle cooked far past al dente.

She had the good grace to look embarrassed. "I'm sorry, Fee. I really was concerned."

"I know." I patted her hand, sighed. "It's okay. You'll find out soon enough anyway. Crew said he OD'd."

Pamela nodded, suddenly the newswoman again. "That much was pretty clear from the way he collapsed," she said. "And I got a peek at the body. Doc owes me." She didn't seem ashamed to admit it.

"But Crew's keeping everyone in town. Does that mean he doesn't think it was accidental?"

Ah, she'd be in the know the second she got to Dr. Aberstock again, so why not? "Skip was taking an experimental painkiller," I said. "But he'd gone off it. Doc found an injection site, though, so Crew thinks someone gave him the drug to push him into OD." I was the daughter of a sheriff telling a reporter about a case. It was official. I was going to hell.

Pamela frowned. "That's a stretch," she said. "Thanks though, I'll check into this drug you mentioned. What's it called?"

I told her about Quexol, though likely bungled the spelling. She wrote it down quickly in her notebook then tucked it into her purse.

"Professional athletes are prone to injury and often have access to excessive amounts of painkillers," she said. "I did a piece once ten years ago just before I moved to Reading. Got me in a lot of hot water, and ultimately fired." She wrinkled her nose like she couldn't give less of a crap. "But I can tell you, it's only gotten worse, not better. So if that young man did OD, he likely did it to himself."

I let her hug me again, this time with more genuine feeling and less discomfort, before waving as she left. I looked down at Petunia who hopped from one front foot to the other, whining softly, rising to my bare feet and heading for the kitchen door, knowing what she was after.

"No pooping on the path," I said, following as she romped out the door and toward the koi pond. Looked up and waved at Pamela who had, for some reason, gone all the way to the corner of the house instead of around the fence again. And stopped, stunned, before hurtling myself after the figure I realized wasn't my friend after all without stopping to think about what I was doing.

It was a woman, though, that much was clear from here. She looked up at me, glasses catching the light, and squealed before taking off around the side of the house. I stumbled over some rocks on the path, cursing and hopping when pain ran up my leg through my bruised toes, bouncing around the corner in a limping run to find the woman had gone.

Had to be the same intruder as this morning. I followed the fence all the way to the street, peeking through the garden gate. The media had already started to gather, vans packing the quiet way even more than Stella's crew had done. I spotted the curly haired man from earlier today, his camera snapping at me. He waved, grinning still, as if someone hadn't died, the jerk. Russell, right? Wasn't that what Skip shouted at him in his heavily drugged and inebriated state?

Whatever. The woman who'd made it onto my property for the last time was gone. I didn't care at this point what she was after, I was done playing Nice Fee. Time to batten down the hatches and seal up Petunia's until Crew got to the bottom of whatever happened to Skip.

With renewed energy and something to do, I returned to the kitchen door to find Petunia waiting for me, grinning like she'd won first prize, a huge, steaming pile of dog poop right in the middle of the path.

CHAPTER FOURTEEN

MY GAG REFLEX HAD obviously grown accustomed to the stink of her poo, because fetching the little garden shovel didn't make me want to throw up like it used to, nor did scooping it with rather practiced efficiency in one quick motion. I was getting good at this. Not that dog poop scooping was going to be an Olympic sport any time soon, but if it ever came up, I'd be a contender.

Petunia, meanwhile, watched with the kind of glassy eyed happiness that was her regular expression, as if having me for a slave was par for her particular puggy course. She followed me when I deposited her offering to the gods of stink in the compost pile and carefully set aside the shovel, her bulging brown eyes seeming to gleam with glee.

"You really need to lay off the sweets," I said, pausing at the door. She farted softly in response before licking her chops, clearly expecting to be fed now that she'd made room in her chubby pug body for more flatulence creating delectables.

The sad truth? She'd likely get them, too. If not from me then from some poor unsuspecting sucker who took her yearning expression at squish face value. And I'd pay the ultimate price for that weakness. Story of my life.

I reached for the door handle, trying not to sigh over this fate life handed me and paused at the sound of raised voices, my amusement at the pug shifting to curiosity when the now familiar sound of Evelyn's piercing words reached me from the depths of the kitchen.

"—you gave him that crap and now look what's happened."

Matt's deeper voice was harder to catch, but the screen was open so when I leaned in to listen I caught his response.

"I had nothing to do with him taking Quexol," he said. "I swear it."

"That's not what Willow told me," Evelyn shot back. "You brought it with you, didn't you?"

The awkward and uncomfortable pause between them made me wonder if they'd left. It was getting darker outside, though, the sun moving behind the mountains, so it was easier to see into the gloom of the kitchen and I caught their still forms next to the bulky stainless steel fridge before Matt spoke again.

"He's been in a lot of pain. I just thought—"

Well now. So Skip's coach had the drug with him.

"I'm telling the sheriff," Evelyn snarled, jabbing him in the chest with one finger. "If you killed Skip, Matt, I'm making sure you go down for it quickly so the rest of us can get the hell out of here."

"How dare you." His voice vibrated with menace. I could feel it from where I stood, breathless, waiting for him to confess. "I've only ever had their best interests at heart."

"Again, not what I heard," Evelyn said, her voice dropping to a hissing whisper. "How's your job security these days, Matt? Anything Skip might have done to jeopardize it?"

There was a lot more going on here than it first appeared, clearly. But rather than gain more information, I lost the chance to keep eavesdropping.

Petunia, her tummy clearly in the way of my snooping, scratched at the door at that exact moment, whining with a yip of insistence to get to where the food was.

Matt and Evelyn both looked up, visibly startled. Knowing my cheeks had to be on fire from getting caught listening to their argument, I pushed the door open and let the pug trot in, following more slowly.

"Mind telling me what all of that was about?" I didn't have the right to ask, of course. I wasn't Crew or a deputy. And from the scrunching of Evelyn's lined face, she knew better than to try to explain herself.

"Excuse me," she said, storming from the room, her high heels clicking on the tile floor. The kitchen door swung silently closed behind her while Matt hesitated, his dark eyes on mine, before he shook his head at me.

"I didn't kill Skip," he said. Then seemed to think better of speaking, shoulders jerking back as if someone pulled his strings tight. He reddened, gaze falling away and he, too, left the room, though with less energy and more emotion trailing after him. Though was it guilt or grief that followed his hasty steps?

I fixed a quick snack for Petunia while I brewed some tea, Mom appearing just as the pug licked the last of the kibble from her bowl. The teapot whistled as she joined me, her hands taking the heavy ceramic from me when my own shook too much to pour.

"I'll take this to Willow for you," Mom said, hot water steaming and releasing the aroma of chamomile from the bag that bobbed to the surface of the porcelain cup. I loved this tea set. It always reminded me of Grandmother Iris with its clear white and faint lines of blue. Took me back to a happier past, sitting in the front room with fresh cookies and milk, listening to the chatter of the ladies on Sunday afternoons. Before I turned into someone I didn't like very much in retrospect and left town in a huff.

Yeah, I was big enough to admit I was a jerk as a teenager.

"I've got it," I said, hugging Mom briefly in thanks as she set the tea and a small plate of cookies on a tray and held it out to me. "I want to talk to her anyway."

Mom sighed. "Of course you do, sweetie." Long suffering, Lucy Fleming, but understanding to the end. Because I was as much my father's daughter as I was hers, and that, I think, was the source of all my problems. I loved my parents. There was a time I just didn't want to turn into them.

Like I had a choice.

The foyer was empty when I passed through it to the stairs. Wherever Crew and Dad had gone off to, same for Daisy and the rest of the guests, I had the entry to myself for a moment. I paused at the bottom of the stairs to steady myself, my trembling slowing and stilling as I breathed in the familiar scent of old wood and polish from the banister, the hint of flowers from the bouquet on the sidebar, the traces of spring that had washed in the door from the beautiful day. Petunia's seemed to breathe with me, an oasis of calm and contentment in the midst of a horror movie. I let the warmth of the last rays of sunlight that made it around the mountains wash me in gold as I gathered my peace and the familiar feel of home.

I blinked, cleared my throat. Shocked to find how much love I had for this place. It was just a building, a collection of furniture and ornaments and memories. But it was *my* place.

This moment of reflection appeared to be exactly what I needed. By the time the grandfather clock boomed its deep tolling of five chimes I was on my way up the stairs to Willow's room with the still hot tea steady on the tray.

CHAPTER FIFTEEN

I KNOCKED SOFTLY AT the white door at the end of the hall on the second floor. While I might not have known which room Willow took, it was easy enough to guess where Daisy would put her. And, it appeared, I was right when movement inside answered, a soft voice responding.

"Who is it?" Definitely Willow.

"Fee," I said. "With some tea, if you'd like."

The door whipped open and she smiled, faint and sad, but welcoming. She immediately stepped aside, her thin hands holding her multicolored wool wrap tightly around her. "Please, come in."

If there was any room in Petunia's that I wished I could claim for my own, it was this one. I loved everything about this suite she'd chosen—that Daisy chose for her. My favorite of all the options in the house, the Green Suite had a spring-like feel to it, with the faintest flowers in the old wallpaper that felt far more chic than worn out, hardwood floors that rich amber tone that could only come with age and love. The four poster queen's velvet upholstered backrest and gossamer curtains that matched those on each of the three large windows begged me to lie down and curl up with the multitude of pillows and handmade quilt of overflowing flowers.

I set the tray down on the small table in the corner, two main windows bracketing the seating area and served Willow as she sank into the arms of the plush chair, its wooden arms curving around her, the padded rests and towering back seeming to swallow the woman in a hug. She appeared so tiny and fragile despite her height, like someone drained her of all her energy and light and left her bereft. I sat across from her, offering her a cookie which she accepted but didn't eat, setting it on the edge of her saucer before straining her teabag and sipping her tea.

"Thank you, Fee," she whispered over it, breathing in the scent. "I needed this." She tried another smile, still tremulous but more substantial at least. "And this visit. There are times I'm surrounded by people but…"

"It has to be easy to feel like you're alone in the job you do," I said.

She nodded then, settling back with the cup in her hands, her dark hair shadowing her as the sun finally set the rest of the way behind the mountains, blue of the sky deepening to the surreal. "Not many people understand real loneliness. And it's hard to talk about it when you're someone like me. It's easy to judge, considering the lifestyle I'm allowed thanks to what I do."

"Because you have it all, right?" I'd always been empathetic, but there was an ease to our connection that felt far more intimate than with anyone I'd ever met. "Perfect husband, perfect job, perfect life?"

She laughed, an unpleasant sound, though a match to her expression and the growing shadows across her face. "Exactly," she said. "All hollow, every bit of it."

The door opened abruptly, Julian entering without knocking. Case in point? He glared at me instantly, though from Willow's sigh his presence and protectiveness wasn't as welcome as he might think.

"That will be all," he snapped at me. "Willow, we need to talk."

Wow. He did *not* just order me around in my place like I was the help.

I had seen Willow's sadness, her kindness with real joy tied in, and even her disillusionment. But I hadn't yet seen her angry. Until now, though just a flicker of it. And again I was reminded that she was far stronger than she appeared.

"Fee and I are having tea," she said without raising her voice. But there was a shift in her tone, a subtle feeling to her that made me feel like I was in the presence of power. I'd thought her charismatic control was in evidence when we'd first met. I had no idea. "We can talk later, Julian."

Either he was accustomed to her and it didn't affect him in the same way or he just didn't care. Because he ignored her subtle warning and went on as if I wasn't there.

"This whole disaster needs to be cleared up immediately," he said. "I don't think you realize the kind of trouble you're in. As your manager and your lawyer, I strongly advise you to keep your mouth shut."

"I didn't kill Skip," she said.

"The spouse is always the prime suspect, you must know that." He glanced at me, as if only then remembering I was there. His eyes dulled, the kind of pit viper expression reminding me he was a lawyer at heart, and I really, really hated lawyers. "You do realize this one is a mouthpiece for the sheriff?"

I looked away rather than answer, my gaze drawn to the bathroom door, gaping open while Willow spoke.

"Stop being ridiculous," she said as my eyes caught the bottle of prescription pills on her countertop and my heart stopped beating for a second.

"Willow," I said, voice more level than I expected. "Were you sharing a room with Skip?" There was no way they were. Her things were distinctive, without a trace of anything masculine to sully her space. And hadn't she said "rooms" when she'd first arrived? That they needed to get settled in their rooms?

"We always take separate spaces," she said as I turned back to meet her eyes. Was that anxiety? So, was it worry she might get caught or that I was judging her?

"That means that's your Vicodin in the bathroom?" I was guessing, of course, the label too small for me to read at this distance. From the twitch of her lips, though, I nailed it. I hated that it sounded as if I was accusing her of something. Lots of people used that painkiller. And there was no proof Vicodin killed Skip. Crew seemed to be on the trail of that new injectable drug, Quexol. So why did the sight of her bottle give me chills? And make me suspect there was more to her story with Skip than I knew, too?

"See?" Julian's snapping tone was paired with a firm hand on my arm trying to pull me out of my seat. I jerked out of his grip and surged to my feet, ready to call him out for daring to lay a finger on me. "I told you. She's not your friend."

Willow sighed, soft and low. I turned to her as she stared into her cup and shrugged.

"Neither are you, Julian," she said. "I'm just your meal ticket and we both know it." He spluttered but she cut him off with a gesture, looking up with fury crackling in her eyes, that iron core showing all over again. "Get out."

"Willow!" He looked back and forth between her and me. "*Dar*ling." How revolting. I didn't know how she could bear to keep him around. I'd have kicked his ass out of my life long ago. But I suppose having someone who *was* the industry in her life was a necessary evil.

"Now, Julian." She set the tea mug aside. "I'm not asking."

He left in a huff after a brief hesitation. I let him go without comment before turning back to Willow, startled to find her standing next to me, eyes staring into mine. Emotionless and without the welcome I'd first seen there. But her expression softened while she sagged before me as if no longer able to hold up a strong front.

"I hurt my back last year," she said. "Doing a stunt for a film. It was stupid." She laughed, a flash of real joy on her face. "It was fun, though. I'd do it again if they'd ever let me. Which they probably never will because I'm a klutz and deserved what I got." She shook her head, softness returning. "I've been in physical therapy for it, but too much activity can make it flare up. I keep the Vicodin for it but I hate taking it."

I nodded, swallowed. "Willow, I'm sorry. Sometimes my curiosity is a curse."

She laughed then and hugged me. "At least you're honest," she said. "That I can respect, Fee. But I am tired, if you don't mind."

I hated that we'd lost our rapport, especially since I really didn't want to believe she killed her husband. Though, from what I knew of him—and how much more was likely hidden from the public—did she have cause? I wouldn't doubt it. And felt ill thinking about it further.

I left her to rest, staring out the window into the dying light, and headed downstairs to the sound of Olivia calling for me. Sighing and eye rolling, I made it to the foyer before she pounced on me, eyes bulging, clearly in a panic.

"Someone posted Skip's death live on social media," she choked. "Every press agency in the world is coming to Reading and we're not ready for that kind of attention!"

Because worrying about what the town looked like was the most important thing when a man was murdered.

CHAPTER SIXTEEN

THANKFULLY MOM APPEARED BEFORE Olivia could shake me or fall into a seizure fit or whatever it was she seemed about to do in the face of such pressure. I wondered again, as I had in February when I noted the weariness in her, just how long our tourism-hungry mayor could keep up the kind of pace that seemed to be leading her down the path to a heart attack or an aneurysm or a public breakdown of massive proportions.

I didn't have to handle it alone at least, my mother's firm hands and capable manner diffusing Olivia as she grasped the mayor's shoulder and squeezed kindly, beaming a smile.

"What an excellent opportunity for Reading!" Dear god, did Mom just spew one of Olivia's taglines? The mayor stilled, smiled a little, as my mother guided her into the sitting room and plunked her firmly on the love seat, Petunia hopping up next to her and leaning into her, panting her happiness while Olivia's hands auto-stroked the pug's soft fur. "Olivia, what do we need to do?"

The mayor gaped at Mom a second before swallowing, the glazed look in her eyes snapping to focused determination. "The council," she gasped, trying to lurch to her feet. But Mom stood right in front of her, pinning her in place.

"Great idea," Mom said. "I'll call city hall and have them assembled. An hour, then?"

Olivia sagged back into the seat and, for a heartbeat, her human side showed. All the stress and anxiety and guilt and longing appeared in little flashes of emotion that seemed to ripple beneath her skin in a crashing tide of impending doom. I gaped at the obvious pressure cracks that showed under the surface of who she showed the world and threw a worried glance at my mother who just beamed down at Olivia with steady confidence.

Amazing to observe the slow recovery, the shift from all that oppressive emotion into calm and collection. How just the supportive and judgement free energy that radiated from my mother seemed to draw out Olivia's panic and ease her into calm.

"Thank you, Lucy," Olivia said, sounding like a human being and not a politician. "That will be fine. I'll make a few calls to some of the local businesses to prepare them."

"And I'll check with the lodge," Mom said, offering Olivia her hand and guiding her to her feet, "to see if they've fixed the gas leak issue."

"Excellent." The mayor nodded to my mother with a pleasant smile then to me as if nothing had happened and walked out of the room, fishing in her pocket for her phone. Only to turn back to the two of us and nod, not noticing Matt descending the stairs behind her. "Well done, you two," she said, whatever that meant. The fact we didn't freak out on her? Or try to shut her down? Maybe. "I know I can count on both of you. We're in this to win it, right?"

I wasn't expecting the snort of derision from Matt as he paused and met my gaze with his own full of wry amusement.

"You sound like a football coach," he said.

She turned to him, nodded. "I could use some pointers then," she said. Her phone rang before he could respond and she lunged from the room, hissing orders to whoever was on the other end.

"Can I trouble you for coffee, Lu?" Matt's humbleness was such a switch from Julian's arrogance I instantly reacted, Mom beside me, the three of us heading for the kitchen. He seemed quite at ease, though grief lingered, and I let my mother—his former principal—handle the coffee prep as I guided the coach back out and into the dining room instead, seating him next to the big hutch full of Grandmother Iris's old china and pulling up a chair next to him.

His big fingers toyed with a folded white napkin, the tables laid out for tea service they wouldn't have to serve for a while if my B&B continued to host a murder investigation. "He was a good guy, once," Matt said. Cleared his throat and looked startled as if surprised he'd spoken out loud.

"I'm sure he was." My experience with sports jocks in high school begged to differ. But Willow obviously saw something in him that was worth hanging onto, so I gave Skip Anderson the benefit of the doubt.

"Not entirely good, though." Matt choked on a laugh as Mom arrived and handed him coffee, sitting on the other side of the sorrowful man, patting his hand gently. He nodded his thanks for the coffee or the kindness, I didn't know which one.

"Matt," Mom said. "I know you have loyalty to Skip. I remember what he was like when I was still teaching, though. Don't you?"

"I do, Lu," he said. "He could be a bully and he hated school. But he was loyal to his team and from what I saw he was good to Willow." Matt hung his head. "And I loved that kid, Lucy, despite his failings. Because we all have them, one way or another."

"True enough," Mom said. "I'm so sorry to see you wrapped up in this, Matt. I've missed talking to you since you left with Skip."

He nodded, wiped at his cheeks in haste as tears escaped his dark eyes. He stared down into the coffee Mom gave him, hands clasped before him on the table, the napkin in a sorry state in his big grip. "It's been a hell of a ride, one I wouldn't trade for anything despite missing being home, teaching the local team. But the chance to go with Skip was just too tempting. And it went well for a long time, a lot of years. It's just that all those concussions, he kept getting worse. I wanted him to take a season off but the doctors cleared him. But this last one." He shook his head, face grim. "It was bad, really bad."

I didn't follow football, but I did vaguely recall hearing Skip had been hurt last season. "But he played this year?"

"He did. Shouldn't have." Matt met my eyes at last, his full of anger. "He was struggling. The team was going to cut him because he was in trouble. We all saw the writing on the wall. So he drugged up as much as he could to kill the pain and got out there every game." He sounded like he thought that kind of dedication had to count for something. I just thought it sounded idiotically stubborn and dangerous.

"Was he going to lose his position on the team, Matt?" And with Skip's career over, wouldn't his coach's go with it?

"It didn't matter anymore," Matt said, so much grief in his voice I could barely make him out. "If the game didn't kill him, the painkillers would have. Did, I guess."

Mom made a soft sound of sorrow, covering one of his hands with her little ones.

"I wish that were the case," Crew's soft voice interrupted. I looked up, startled, we all did, to find the sheriff standing in the doorway of the dining room, looking grim. "But the report just came back and it's as I feared. Skip died of an OD brought on by a massive injection of Quexol."

Matt's lower lip quivered. "I should disclose I have some with me. But the bottle is full. I never used it."

Crew sighed, shrugged. "I'll still need to question you," he said. "And confiscate the drug. For now, though, things aren't looking good for accidental overdose." Of course they weren't. "He has no other puncture wounds or places of entry for the dose of Quexol. And the location of injection paired with the angle of entry makes it almost impossible for him to have administered it himself." Naturally. "The amount that was found in his system exceeds any normal dosage, likely an entire bottle injected at once."

Which meant, as I feared, Petunia's wasn't opening to the public any time soon.

Crew confirmed it. "It's pretty clear at this point Skip Anderson was murdered."

CHAPTER SEVENTEEN

I STIRRED THE POT of spaghetti sauce simmering on the gas burner and tried to shake off the feeling that Petunia's had become a prison. It certainly felt that way, made worse by the fall of darkness. While the sound of their presence was muffled by the thick walls of the B&B, the flashing and glaring lights of the media gathered outside and the volume of voices talking over each other as reporters went live with my precious bed and breakfast in the background—I'd seen enough watching a few news channels as I cooked dinner to feel even more empathy for Willow and the public life she led—made it impossible to ignore the fact any kind of normalcy was out of the question.

I hoped our food stores would hold up because we weren't leaving without being badgered and hounded by the press any time soon.

Crew had almost immediately confiscated the front sitting room for his interrogations. "I can't take them past that circus to the station for questioning," he told me in a low voice as Jill escorted Matt to Grandmother Iris's antique sofa and stood over him. "I just don't have the room to house everyone. And going back and forth will be a logistical nightmare." He was right. I wasn't arguing. "I'm sorry to do this to you, Fee, but since the suspects are here, I need to use Petunia's."

"It's okay," I said, noting that my dad hovered and watched, brows drawn together, but whether feeling protective of me or needing to interject himself in the case I didn't know. Either way, he wasn't going anywhere, I could tell. "I'm used to it by now, I think."

Crew's little smile was grim but lit his blue eyes. "You're okay? Really?"

I nodded, exhaled. "Just hurry up and figure it out before I beat you to it this time."

I really knew how to push his buttons. Crew's nostril flare and loss of amusement told me I'd stepped over the line when I was just trying to be funny. Because foot in mouth seemed to be my most common form of communication with him.

"If you could keep your head down and, if you can manage it, stop feeding Pamela information." He snapped that off before spinning, shoulders stiff, and stalking away while my own temper sparked. I'd managed to bruise his little boy ego, had I? Did he think that parting shot was going to get to me?

I jabbed the wooden spoon into the pot of bubbling sauce, splattering the front of my apron with my irritated enthusiasm. Well, I guess he knew what he was doing after all. If only he could translate that into police work my B&B wouldn't feel like someone smothered it in bars and locks.

Mom firmly took the spoon from me and tasted my attempt at food before shoving me aside with one hip and reaching for spices over the stove, adding this and that as she spoke.

"You're lost in here," she said, turning to offer Petunia a slice of pineapple from the fruit salad she'd been assembling before straightening, wiping her hands with a professional air on her apron before fixing me with those green eyes that were my eyes. "And you're in my way. Not to mention how unsanitary it is to have Petunia in here while we're cooking."

Mom should have known better. Keeping the pug out of the kitchen was actually impossible. Honestly, having her here *was* kind of against state rules. Somehow, though, Grandmother Iris had forged an agreement with the Department of Health, something to do with a Grandfather clause she'd negotiated, though I never looked that particular gift horse in the mouth.

Besides, Mom's statement had nothing to do with the pug's presence and everything to do with getting me out of her hair. "Fine." I removed my own apron and set it aside, sinking to the stool at the counter, planning to mope a bit before trying to find a way to make myself useful that didn't involve irritating Crew further. But Dad's appearance just stirred up my curiosity all over again.

I actually perked as he paused next to Mom and helped himself to a slice of garlic bread she'd just pulled from the oven. She tried to smack him but it was a half-hearted effort. My stomach growled at the scent of toast and butter and cheesy garlic goodness as Dad spoke around a bite.

"We need to plug some leaks, Fee," he said. "Jill caught a reporter sneaking around the Munroe property and the fence."

My jaw tightened, headache starting in my right temple. "Not sure what we can do about it." Did I really just sound that whiny? Well, I wasn't exactly in the kind of get up and go mood that maybe I should have been.

"Jill and Robert have their hands full with the media," Dad said, a bit softer and with the kind of gentleness that irritated me in the state I was in. "Crew asked me to help, and I'm asking you."

Mom paused, looked up at Dad with the wooden spoon dripping, her face dark and lips tight. "He did not deputize you, John."

I gaped at Dad who looked suddenly uncomfortable.

"The kid's in a bind, Lucy," Dad said, apology in his tone while my mother turned from him with a sniff that spoke volumes.

"You just run along and play at being a police officer again, then, dear," she said.

"Now, Lu," Dad started. And froze as she spun back on him, little body vibrating.

"You listen to me, Johnathan Albert Campbell Fleming," she said. "I've been very patient. I even helped you scratch that itch of the cop you were in February when that boy was killed. Did I complain?" Sauce splashed as she plunged the spoon in to the pot and stirred with vigor. "Not a word. But I'll tell you right now, if you make this a habit, you and I are having a long conversation about the promises you made to me when you—you, John!—chose to retire."

Wow. Gulp. I had no idea there was this kind of tension between them about Dad's job.

He met my gaze with a guilty look, clearly uncomfortable. "It's just until the state troopers get here," he said.

Mom grunted something that wasn't appropriate for polite company or small children and fell silent. Even I knew better than to try to talk to her in this particular mood. Instead, I gestured at Dad to follow me and he joined me, shoulders slumped, out the door into the garden, Petunia following me, oddly, despite the fact there was food to be had in the kitchen. Even she must have sensed Mom wasn't in a generous frame of mind.

"She'll be okay," Dad sighed into the darkness, the outside light clicking on as our motion activated it. The matching one on the carriage house flickered but didn't turn on, leaving most of the garden in shadow.

"Are you two having trouble?" I would hate that. Utterly hate it. No way my parents were those parents. How could I have missed it?

But Dad dispelled my worries, hugging me briefly. "She's right and she's been a saint. I'm just an old fool who can't let go of something that didn't do me a bit of good for a lot of years, Fee." He pushed me gently away, sadly smiling down at me. "You wondered why I did my best to keep you as far from law enforcement as I could? It wasn't because I didn't think you could do it. Or because I worried you'd get hurt."

He was not going to trigger tears. I refused to cry as he went on. Refused.

"It's the toll it takes on the family, kid," he said. "I lucked out with your mom. She picked me, bless her, knew what she was getting into. I never deserved her or the way she just put up with me."

"Dad." I choked out that word, cleared my throat.

He kissed my forehead and let me go. "She's been after me to travel. I think that's a great idea, don't you?" He inhaled, exhaled, a gusty sigh, grinning then. "Forget the fence. Let security deal with it." He winked and turned, going back inside, and I stood there in the dark and hugged my pug while I watched through the windows as my father embraced and then kissed my mom like they were twenty again.

And cried, at last, in silence and the night, for the amazing parents I was lucky to call my own.

Almost missed, through my tears, the light over the carriage house turning on. And spun, heart pounding, fury flaring, my pug quickly dropped at my feet before I ran at full speed through the path to the fence and tackled with a full body throw the intruder who tried to flee. Not this time. Not on my watch.

CHAPTER EIGHTEEN

BREATH WHOOSHED FROM MY lungs as I carried the other person to the ground, the soft and slightly squishy body oofing a gust of air out while I landed on top of the woman. Petunia arrived a moment later, huffing and puffing, throwing herself into the mix as she pounced on my prisoner.

I panted when I flipped her over and looked down into the scared face of the young woman from earlier today, the same one who escaped me around the corner of the house. There was no escape for her this time. I grabbed my phone from my back pocket and dialed Crew as the woman squirmed but didn't try to get up.

"Fee." His clipped response at the third ring told me he was irritated. Well, poor baby. "I'm in the middle of an—"

"I caught an intruder in the backyard," I snapped back. "Mind sending a real cop to finish the job I started?"

He swore softly and hung up. At me or at the situation I was in? Honestly, I couldn't care less which. So. Over. It.

I heard the kitchen door slam as I stood and grabbed the woman's arm, jerking her to her feet. Maybe manhandling her wasn't the best option, but I'd had a hell of a day and she was on my last nerve. Her glasses flashed, catching the light she'd triggered with her appearance, blocking briefly the view of her wide, frightened eyes, her ponytail coming loose, her thin hair cascading over her shoulders. Wait, I knew her from somewhere, didn't I? That brown cardigan, the practical shoes. The acne and frumpy skirt. Where had I met her before?

Dad appeared at a run, Crew right behind him, the two of them coming to a jarring halt when I spun her around and made her face them.

"Here you go," I snarled. "One intruder. You're freaking welcome."

Crew didn't comment, handing Dad a set of handcuffs. My father raised his eyebrows at me but remained silent as he shackled the young woman and Crew addressed her.

"This is private property and off limits to anyone at the moment," Crew said, gruff and doing his best to intimidate. I wanted to laugh in his face, I was that wound up, but it worked on the girl.

"I'm sorry," she blubbered, face wet with tears, shaking in Dad's grip. "I just wanted to make sure Willow was okay." She looked up at me. "Is she okay, Fee?"

She knew me? And thought she did well enough to use my nickname, clearly. "She's fine," I said. "Do you know her?"

The girl beamed then, nodded, her whole attitude changing in a flash. "She's amazing, isn't she? I'm her biggest fan." She wriggled a little as if in delight I asked. "I was so worried about her, she's had such trouble with that husband of hers lately." Her voice dropped, conspiratorial and only for my ears as though she forgot she was in handcuffs and Dad and Crew were there to take her away. "When I heard he died I knew Willow was finally safe. But I needed to know she's okay." Her face shone with adoration.

And we had a nut job. But as she turned from me to look at Crew, I had an epiphany and blurted out what I remembered before I could censor myself.

"You work at the nursing home." That's where I knew her from. "You gave me Grandmother Iris's box that day I came to pick up her things." Wow, it felt like years ago now.

She nodded to me, snuffled some snot, smiling like she hadn't expected me to recall our meeting. "Mila Martin," she said. "You remembered me." Shy suddenly, and rather pleased. That made me nervous for some reason.

Crew didn't seem to notice or care. "Bring her inside," he said. "Let's have a little chat, shall we?"

I could have stayed in the kitchen with Mom. Should have, maybe. But she had the recently reappeared Daisy at her side to keep her company, wherever my best friend vanished to all this time. Where had Daisy gone? It didn't matter now as she and Mom whispered over making dinner, so I just waved and carried on, Petunia still following me, into the foyer with Dad, Mila and Crew in the lead.

The hulking bodies of my father and the sheriff almost cut off the reaction Julian and Stella had to Mila's appearance. I caught only the instant vocal protest and had to ease around my dad to see the revulsion Julian displayed and the utter disgust on the director's face.

"That woman isn't allowed to be anywhere near Willow," Julian huffed, jabbing a finger at Mila who cowered next to Dad.

"Did you kill Skip, you nasty little witch?" Stella's accusation made me flinch.

Mila's shaking, the soft wail that escaped her, how she turned and buried her face against my father's chest to protect herself from the two and their accusing hatefulness made me wonder if she was in the throws of guilt or just terrified.

"I take it there's a restraining order against Miss Martin?" Crew sounded tired, frustrated.

"Not that the police seem to take it seriously," Julian snapped. "That *thing* has made threats against Skip and stalked our Willow for years."

"We are friends," Mila whispered just loud enough for me to hear. "Since high school." She met my eyes through the glare of her glasses, her disconnect with reality pretty clear in the glazed and desperate look there.

I actually felt sorry for her.

"You can put this all to a rest and drag her off to prison, Sheriff," Stella said, arms crossing over her chest, judge, jury and executioner written all over her face. "If anyone killed Skip—and is a continuing threat to Willow—it's this psycho stalker."

I ignored the director's tirade, focusing on Mila's reaction. How she winced at every word, the way she trembled and clung to Dad.

"I have a stack of threatening letters in my office back in L.A.," Julian said. "All from that piece of trash. While we don't often agree, I think Stella is right. She had to have done it."

"And, can I ask you two expert detectives exactly how she got close enough to Skip to inject him with enough painkiller to trigger an overdose?" Crew took just the right tone, in my opinion. That kind of lazy, smartass and yet authoritative growl that got everyone's attention. I caught the flash of Dad's hastily suppressed grin as Crew went on. "Right then. If you'd be kind enough to leave the police work to the actual police, I'd be ever so grateful."

Snorty time. Okay, so I was really tired, but still. That was about as close to perfect as he could get. And while I was kind of pissed at him, I could appreciate the brilliance. It even softened me toward him as he gestured to Dad.

"Please escort Miss Martin to one of the rooms and make sure she stays there until I'm ready to talk to her."

Dad nodded, led the weeping Mila away who muttered over and over, "That's not what happened."

Julian and Stella both left in a huff, marching upstairs after them. I sighed and shook my head, feeling the bruises that would likely form shortly from my tackle and the impact of the day finally getting to me.

"Nice," I said. "You practice that speech in the mirror?" Again, I meant to be funny. Honestly, just a joke. Intended for a bit of camaraderie, a flash of banter, a back and forth of joking to soften the mood and maybe our feelings for each other.

Instead, Crew's face darkened and he glared, fists on hips, brow furrowed.

"For the last time, Fiona Fleming," he snarled, "stay out of police business." He huffed softly before hammering the final nail into his own coffin. "You want to be helpful? Go make me a sandwich."

Oh. *Snap.* No. No he did *not*.

Crew seemed to realize he'd gone too far. Or that what he'd said might have sounded right in his head before he said it but the connotations were so off the grid of anything resembling decency and respect he'd flung himself over the side and into the deepest ocean of misogyny he could find without a lifejacket.

We stared at each other in utter silence a long moment, him slowly crumbling in apology he didn't speak out loud and me going more and more rigid by the moment, cold spiking a chill to the center of my soul.

With absolutely nothing to say, I turned and walked away.

CHAPTER NINETEEN

I DIDN'T MAKE IT to the kitchen door. Instead, I came to an abrupt halt at the sight of Carter carrying a platter of garlic bread into the dining room. He paused as he spotted me, looking so startled I'm sure the expression on my face had to reflect the conversation I'd just had with Crew. Or lack of one.

"Your mother recruited me," Carter said. "I hope that's okay?"

"Aren't you supposed to be guarding someone?" Yeah, that was nasty and uncalled for but he didn't hold it against me. Instead, his brow furrowed, his gaze flashing to the foyer and back again.

"Everything okay, Fee? Do you need help with anything?"

The way he said it instantly made me feel better. Because there was a threat in that offer, an open invitation to do harm to anyone who might have slighted or belittled me. And while I'd never take him up on it, knowing not all men were utter dicks like, apparently, the sheriff of Curtis County, Vermont, lightened my mood considerably.

And, in all honesty, I had to cut myself some slack. I'd been through a lot today and was shocked it had only been a few hours since Skip died in my lap.

"Thank you." I tried to take the platter from him but he bowed in a courtly fashion instead, good nature returning, that handsome face rugged in all the right ways. "I'm fine, I promise."

"Good to hear it," he said. "If you're up to it, your mother is looking for you." He talked about her like he revered her. Another tick in the boxes of hell yeah for Carter Melnick. Maybe I wasn't such a bad judge of character after all.

I left him to deliver the food to the sideboard and joined Mom, finding her dishing up sauce over noodles while Petunia snuffled in her bowl, likely snarfling down a serving of her own.

Before I could tell Mom what Crew said, she looked up, smiled and dropped what she was doing before leaning across the counter and offering me a sandwich.

A. Sandwich. No. Not my Mom. She could not be in on Crew's little jab of be a good girl and stay in the kitchen...?

From the look on her face she instantly realized she'd done something wrong and hesitated before setting the plate back on the counter. "I know you don't like spaghetti," she said. "So I made you this instead."

Of course she did. Of course this was a kindness, a gesture of motherly love, not a jab or a jibe or a hurtful attempt to stop me from being me. How could I have thought otherwise of the amazing Lucy Fleming? I hugged her and pulled myself together before smiling at her while Carter rejoined us, helping himself to a slew of plates and then disappearing again.

"That boy," she said, "is a godsend. He's served, you can tell? Thank goodness because if Daisy dropped one more plate..." My mother sighed, leaned against the counter. "I sent her back to help that film crew she's working with. Poor dear. I think she misses Petunia's." The sound of voices outside the kitchen door told me people were starting to gather for dinner. I wasn't sure if Mom's delicious dinner would do the trick for big shot L.A. folk but it was good enough for me.

"Mom," I said, now confused by her sandwich offer. "I love your spaghetti."

"Really?" She hesitated, head cocked to one side, looking more like my pug at the moment than she probably would have appreciated. "I distinctly remember you saying you hated spaghetti. And throwing it in the sink."

Ah. Memories. Like the bane of my existence. "I was seventeen," I said, voice small and embarrassed to even open my mouth. "Dad and I had a fight. It wasn't the spaghetti, Mom. It was my life."

She flinched. I watched her face relax into understanding and then perk to forgiveness and acceptance. Because she was that awesome.

"Besides," I said. "Dad made dinner that night, not you. So if anyone's spaghetti earned my wrath, it was his."

Her eyes twinkled at the offer of an escape and she laughed. "Of course. Now I remember. He had a thing for kidney beans." She wrinkled her nose and snorted. "That man. I could shake him sometimes." She met my eyes and her face settled into knowing wisdom and the steady offer of return to our new normal if that was what I wanted. Coward, I accepted, though I had to admit this really wasn't a good time to talk about why I left Reading. Maybe someday, but not today. "Something happen with Crew?"

Now how did she guess that? Because Mom was brilliant. I quickly imparted the conversation in my grumpiest crank humor and she gasped before her eyes narrowed. Mom grabbed the plate with my sandwich on it and offered it to Petunia. Startled, the pug snorted on it before my mother jerked it away again, a mischievous look on her face.

Wait, hang on. She wasn't about to do what I thought she was about to do? And I was going to let her, oh yes I was.

"I'm sure Crew must be *starving*," she said. "I'll be right back."

It honestly wasn't that big a deal. Petunia snorted on me all the time. Farted, drooled, you name it, she shared it willingly with anyone who came in close contact. It was the idea of what my mother was up to. The deliberate delivery of pug bodily fluids to an unsuspecting victim who should know better than to be mean to me. I really should have made her come back, but instead I beamed at her as she exited the room with the sandwich on the plate and giggled like a child.

"Who's a good girl?" My pug farted with great happiness despite having no clue she was in on the biggest joke ever, because yes, yes she was all that and more.

Carter made another pass at dinner delivery, the last of the plates disappearing with him. He winked at me on the way out, butt hitting the door, Mom sneaking in past him as he left, a huge and wicked smile on her face.

"He's eating it as we speak," she chuckled. "That'll teach him to tell my daughter to make him a sandwich."

I sank to the stool by the counter, Mom ladling me some spaghetti and a generous helping of sauce, setting it in front of me before dishing up one of her own. A small basket of garlic bread appeared from the oven and she gestured with a fork for me to start.

"I thought maybe you'd like to eat back here," she said. "You've had a rough day, sweetie."

"Thanks, Mom," I sighed over the delicious smells. "You're the best, you know that?"

"Of course," she said. Paused and spoke again with soft sympathy. "You do know he likely didn't mean it the way it came out, right? Men have this dumb way of blurting things when they're under stress that doesn't sound the same out loud as it does in their silly heads."

My mother, Oh Wise Woman. "I know," I said, toying with a noodle. I was hungry but just not yet in the mood to eat. Weird but true. "He makes me crazy sometimes."

Mom laughed. "You just described your father, Fee. From day one he drove me around the bend and back again."

"Wait, it wasn't love at first sight?" I finally took a bite and let the fabulousness that was my mother's cooking fill my mouth a moment before chewing and swallowing. "I thought you chased him down and made him marry you because he was your true love?" At least, that was the way Dad always told it.

Mom snorted, nibbling her garlic bread. "Oh, please. That man has a massive sense of his own importance that has nothing to do with reality. The truth was, he needed someone to take care of him, the poor dear, or he would have been alone his entire life, miserable and lost."

Nice to hear her side of events at last in a grin inducing snark delivery. "Go on, I'm listening."

"He was a pain in my butt, I'll tell you," she said. "Chasing me around, making moon eyes at me, pretending he wasn't interested but always telling the girls he liked me. Silly fool." She was actually blushing. "I only asked him to go out with me so he'd stop pestering my friends."

"Mom, you make him sound creepy, you know that, right?" I grinned around more pasta.

"No," she said. "Just pathetic." We laughed together but she settled, her teasing turning to real warmth. The kind of look I recognized when she talked about Dad. The love never ending look. Made me choke up a bit. "He was so genuine, Fee. So honest and endearing and absolutely terrible at courting me. He tried harder than anyone else and just didn't have the knack. He said and did the wrong things more often than not. I almost walked." She nodded abruptly once after a moment's thought as if making the decision to stay all over again. "But when I finally decided to look past his mistakes and the words and actions that he'd been raised by, I instead saw the intent behind everything. And his intentions were always the best."

A huge weight lifted off my shoulders and I slumped, sad and happy and a mix of feelings that didn't make much sense as she went on.

"So, I made a choice. To give John the benefit of the doubt every time, to stop choosing to get mad and instead see past what he said to what he meant. And because of that, I married him. That attitude has kept us happy and talking and together for the last thirty-two years."

I had no idea. "You're a better woman than I am, Mom."

"I doubt that very much." She leaned in and kissed my cheek. "You might be more like John than you are me, but you can do whatever you choose to do. And if that means seeing past the flubs of someone like Crew Turner or the sweet talk and charisma of the Carter Melnicks in the world, it's up to you."

So she noticed that, did she? Not much got past Lucy Fleming.

She was right, though. Ryan had that kind of easy going sweetness to him, just like Carter. Was I falling for the same guy all over again?

Before I could comment, Mom's gaze left mine, flickering over my shoulder and she gasped, one hand pressing to her chest. I spun, heart in my throat along with my spaghetti as it rose in response to my heightened fear. Turned to sudden rage at the sight of the paparazzo Russell creeping by my back door.

With red closing in around my vision and Mom calling after me, I stomped across the tile with ill intent, positive if I got ahold of him Crew would have a second murder on his hands.

CHAPTER TWENTY

FORTUNATELY FOR RUSSELL, HE was more agile than I was at the moment and managed to evade me, though he did nothing to try to escape, snapping pictures of me as I lunged for him, clicking more of the kitchen past the door.

"Get the hell off my property." That sounded about right, growled in Dad's low and threatening cop voice.

But Russell was made of sterner stuff than the average human. I should have known that a mere command would grant me a grin and more photographing. "Make me, sweetheart."

As was extremely apparent, the last eight hours or so of my life hadn't been stellar and having an arrogant jerkwad of a photographer stick a camera in my face and call me sweetheart while basically ignoring my right to privacy was pretty much the perfect culmination of events.

The redhead in me snapped, a shriek building in my chest to the point I am positive, given opportunity, means and motive wouldn't have been remotely in question.

But before I could fly completely off the handle and go all Fleming on his ass, he lowered his camera and winked.

"Before you bust a gut and call the cops in on this," he said, "I've got some information you might find interesting."

"For a price," I snarled.

He shrugged, lowering the camera further. "Maybe," he said. "Or maybe not, if you're nice to me. Skip wasn't my biggest fan and the feeling was mutual. But Willow always played fair. So maybe I owe her one or two."

That settled my temper a bit, but not enough to give him a free ride. "So tell the cops," I said. "If your information is important."

"Didn't say that," he said. "Just that it's interesting. Figured you could pass it along for me and keep me out of the mess."

"Let me guess," I said. "Restraining order?"

He laughed then, tipping his camera at me. "You're smarter than you look, Red."

Grumble, snarl, growl, argh. "What is it, then? I don't have all night."

Russell hesitated, shrugged. Opened his mouth. Only to stiffen then spin and run for it. I stared in shock, frozen by his sudden vanishing act, hearing the screen door slam, feet pounding past me, Carter in hot pursuit of the paparazzo while I stood there in stunned silence.

Something fluttered to the ground at my feet. I bent, retrieved the business card. Randy Russell. Some kind of cheesy tagline that made me wince. And a phone number and website address.

I looked up from it, Carter triggering the light over the carriage house. I really did have to plug the hole in that fence. Still a bit stunned by the whole event, I turned back to the house and, on my way past, dumped the card on the compost pile.

And that was what I thought of the photographer's offer to help.

Carter came jogging back and I held the door for him, but he waited for me to go inside first. A perfect gentleman. Mom spotted us together and, clearing her throat, exited the kitchen with a little smile, leaving us alone with the sadly watchful Petunia.

"You're okay?" He was fuming still, vibrating from the chase. "That guy, he thinks he's outside the law. Damned paparazzi."

"He was there this afternoon when Skip died." I sat again, my legs wobbly. I really needed to lie down. All of the stress and adrenaline rushes had finally knocked the wind out of me.

"I'm not surprised," Carter said. "Randy probably laughed when Skip passed away."

Yikes. "They hated each other that much?"

"Randy used to track Willow, but one night Skip got ahold of him outside a club and beat the crap out of him." Wow, nice guy. "Ever since, Randy's made it his mission to destroy Skip. Posts all kinds of private photos about them. He's a menace."

"Good to know," I said. "He tried to offer me some inside info."

"I wouldn't trust a word he says." Carter's anger faded and he sank down next to me, concern in his beautiful dark eyes. He really was delicious to look at.

Surely he had a soul, something my ex didn't possess? I was positive I saw one behind that gaze. "Fee, you look exhausted."

"Thanks." I made a wry face. "Just what a girl likes to hear after the day from hell."

He touched my cheek ever so gently before dropping his hand and actually blushing. Wow. "I just meant... you should take care of yourself. That was horrible, what you went through. I wish I could take the experience away for you."

Heat rushed through me as I leaned closer, Carter matching me. "He's not my first dead body," I said, meaning it as a joke but unable to stop the hitch that added a sad little tremor to my voice.

Carter's big hand settled over mine. "You're pretty brave, you know. I'd be a basket case."

As if. "Thanks." Um, that came out a bit breathy. Didn't help he was so close, his face now inches from mine. How did that happen? Such intensity in those eyes, so much caring and gentleness for a man who dished out violence for a living.

I have no idea if he would have kissed me or I would have kissed him or anything else that could have evolved from that long, warm moment of just staring into Carter's eyes. I didn't get the chance to find out. Because as I sat there, dreamily lost in his deep brown gaze, the kitchen door swung open and Crew walked in.

I'd done nothing wrong. It wasn't like Crew and I had anything even remotely resembling a relationship building between us. If anything, we were screwing up enough in our communication with each other that gold sweater would have gone to waste in my closet.

So why did I jerk back from Carter with guilt smothering the heated happiness of the last minute or so? Crew's face went from open questioning to flat emptiness in about a heartbeat before he nodded to me and then to Carter, spun and left the room like he hadn't come in here for a reason.

Or tried to. Mom was already on her way back in and, with a firm hand on his chest, pushed him backward, protesting, until the door swung shut behind her.

"Thanks for the help," I said. Carter nodded, stood.

"Get some rest," he smiled. "You earned it, Fee." When Carter turned, I saw him purposely make eye contact with Crew who didn't budge an inch. Because boys were idiots and their hormones made them Neanderthal thugs who pounded their chests and thought their stupid displays of manhood impressed anyone.

Yeah, it was that kind of night.

Mom ignored Carter, smiling at me like nothing was wrong. "How was your sandwich, Crew?"

He muttered something under his breath before side stepping her. "I have work to do." This time he managed to escape while Mom sighed at me.

"What?" My turn to make an exit. Before she gave me a hard time for something that I was already starting to beat myself up over.

CHAPTER TWENTY-ONE

WORK KEPT ME BUSY into the wee hours, a welcome distraction. I'd unplugged the phone, letting the message service take my calls after it rang incessantly starting about two seconds after I got back from the parade. But I really needed to do some damage control and, as I sighed over the maxed-out list that clogged my phone's inbox, not to mention the email flood that washed away any chance I had to sleep in the next several hours, I let myself become absorbed in running Petunia's again.

Speaking of my place's namesake, she curled up next to me on the couch in my living room downstairs, snoring as I settled my laptop on my legs, propped my feet on the coffee table, and sorted through all the pending messages burdening my chugging computer with their demands.

One would think murder would be an excellent deterrent to visiting a cutsie little town like ours, but I'd found just the opposite to be the truth. After the death of Pete Wilkins last July, Petunia's had been busier than ever, as if knowing someone died out back increased interest. And with the murder of Skip Anderson, it appeared like the lull I'd experienced the last little while was officially over. I had people messaging me to come stay immediately in rather insistent language that set me off before making me sigh. I finally had to create a standard "closed for business at the moment" email that I truly hated to send, at least to cover the next week. Because who knew how long the party would go on upstairs? Surely I wouldn't be so lucky as I had been on Valentine's Day and have everything wrap up in less than twenty-four hours.

Nope. Not this time, Fleming.

After a week, well, it would likely turn into a free for all and my few empty dates were filled almost immediately with a waiting list piling up in frightening fashion. The rest of the night was spent apologizing and booking into the following year. If I had the time and was smart about it, I'd buy another place and expand. I knew Olivia would have loved that and was likely planning something of her own, despite the 150 new rooms at the lodge. It sounded like most tourists wanted to stay right here in Reading. There was an excellent chance there would be a few illegal operations fire up before summer hit, and so be it.

The Munroe's next door had never sold. I let myself sit back a moment and wonder how much work it would take to renovate it and make it a sister property to mine. But even as the idea crossed my mind, I shook my head at my own ridiculousness—and the very thought of setting foot in that place again—and smiled down at the snoring pug who chose that moment to fart in blissful unawareness.

"We're good, aren't we, pug?"

Weren't we? I wondered.

The grandfather clock upstairs chimed midnight before I was done, and I only finished a moment before Dad walked down the stairs, the laptop warm on my legs, the lid clicking softly into place as I looked up and tried to smile. Everything was kind of blurry, the headache that had started a few hours ago full blown and I groaned loud enough to wake Petunia who started upright with a snort, blinking at me like I'd woken her on purpose.

Dad didn't say anything. He crossed to me, sat on the coffee table and handed me two pills and a glass of water. "You're going to need these."

I downed the ibuprofen with a quick swig and nodded. "Is Crew still interrogating people?"

"He just finished with the main group." Dad sounded reserved but soft around the edges. Almost nostalgic without the normal gruffness that colored his tone. "He did a good job, Fee. He's turning into a hell of a sheriff."

"Good to know," I grumbled. "Anything else?"

Dad laughed. "Not on the Crew Turner Fan Club list anymore, kiddo?"

Grunt.

"The only hold out is Mila Martin," he said. "We were thinking you might give it a go. If you're interested?"

"We" my ass. "Why should I be?" Yeah, I was being a baby. So what?

"She's your collar," he said, standing up, mild manner still in place. "And neither of us could get anything out of her. She seemed to open up to you, though. Just thought I'd ask."

The painkillers were already kicking in and the irony of what I just took—while not Vicodin—wasn't lost on me. "Fine," I said. "I'll help. But I'm not making anyone a damned sandwich."

Dad's frown of confusion told me he had no idea what I was talking about.

"Never mind," I sighed, setting my laptop on the coffee table, my pug hopping down as Dad helped me to my feet. "Let's see what Mila has to say."

It was pretty clear from the look on Crew's face he wasn't in on Dad's plan as I'd expected. But when he paused his interrogation to give my father a hard time, Mila looked up from where she huddled in silence on the sofa and met my eyes. And beamed a smile at me.

"Fee!" She gestured for me to join her. That shut Crew up long enough for me to make an I told you so face despite those words not changing hands and sat with her as he scowled at my childishness or my presence or just because he liked to scowl. Take your pick.

"Mila." I accepted her hand as she squeezed mine, leaning in to me, Petunia sitting at her feet and looking up at her like she didn't know what to do. Odd the dog didn't jump up like she always did. "You need to tell us what you were doing outside."

"I already did." She pouted a bit, but at Crew, not me. "He's mean," she whispered. "Is he always this mean?"

I didn't comment, but boy did I want to. "Mila, you know you're not supposed to be here. Why did you come?"

She looked down at our hands twined together. "Willow's in danger," she said. "Or, she used to be."

"From you." Crew needed to shut the hell up. This was my interrogation, thanks.

But Mila shook her head and finally spoke to him, though when she met his eyes she looked away immediately, as if he scared her. "No," she said. "Not me. I was trying to save her."

"From who, Mila?" I was pretty sure I knew the answer.

"From that monster she married." Mila's face crumpled. "She wouldn't admit it to anyone, but I know. I saw. He beat her," she whispered those last three words before her voice rose in volume again while my heart skipped a beat. "And I have proof."

CHAPTER TWENTY-TWO

WHILE I WASN'T SURPRISED, to be honest, silence reigned long enough for Willow to fly down the stairs in a flurry and hurtle herself across the foyer and to the entry to the sitting room. The panic and hurt on her face told me she'd not only been listening in the whole time, but that Mila was right.

"Please," she sobbed once before clutching a shaking hand to her mouth, staring at Mila with those huge eyes full of pain. "*Please.*"

"I can't keep quiet," Mila said, sounding the more sane of the two, oddly, nodding with firm purpose to Willow before meeting my eyes again. Such determination and loyalty. Could she have killed Skip after all? Well, the motive was clearly there, but means and opportunity? "I've loved Willow since high school." She said it like it wasn't anything that was a secret or a big deal, but it was clear the kind of love she meant wasn't just friendly. "She was two years ahead of me and was the only person who was kind to me. She used to defend me against Skip and the guys who would bully me." She beamed a smile at Willow who crumpled while Dad gently guided the star into the room and sat her in a chair where she seemed to collapse in on herself.

Whether she felt remorse over speaking up or not, Mila went on.

"It was Skip who got the restraining order." I wasn't so sure about that. Mila's passion burned in her and I could see how such delusion could lead Willow to be afraid enough to ask the courts for protection. "It was all his fault we couldn't be together."

"Oh, Mila," Willow whispered.

"It's true!" She tried to stand, but I gently held her in place and when she turned toward me again, that dreamy kind of adoration was back. "It's all right now, though," she said. "He's dead, and good riddance."

I knew what everyone in the room was thinking because I was thinking the exact same thing. "Mila," I said. "What proof do you have of the abuse?" Forget the fact Willow might hold the question against me. It might not be the kind of thing the star wanted known publically, but it was an excellent motive for murder and had to come out. As much as I liked and respected Willow, if she was Skip's killer she needed to face her punishment.

Though, if a man ever hit me? Yeah, no one would ever find the body.

Mila tipped her hip, looking down at her pocket. "My phone," she said.

I divested her of it while Crew tried to take it from me but I dodged him and smiled at Mila while the screen came to life. "Password?"

"2025," she said. "Of course."

Willow's latest science fiction movie title. Naturally. I tapped out the numerals and clicked on her picture folder. One was clearly marked "WILLOW" and seemed to hold the bulk of the images on her phone. But another said "PROOF" and I hovered a finger over it, waiting.

"Yes," Mila said, eager and near panting with her need to share now. "That one."

I almost handed it over to Crew after all. My heart hurt for the horrified and despair riddled woman across the room who turned her face away, quietly weeping. But my inborn sense of curiosity— thanks, Dad—wouldn't let me stop. And, for some reason, instead of trying to take the phone again, Crew sat on the arm of the sofa and looked with me as I clicked the folder.

"That was in Las Vegas last year," Mila said about the amazingly sharp photo of the limousine, clearly night time with lights shining overhead, Skip hulking threateningly over Willow who cowered as his hand froze in its descent toward her face. The second image was the impact, the third a bit blurry as Willow fell.

"My hands were shaking," Mila said and I looked up to find her weeping. "That's why it's out of focus." Her excitement hadn't left her but she didn't seem happy about it. More as if she'd sat on this far too long.

My hands were trembling too actually and I had to draw a deep breath as I clicked the next image. This one was sunny, bright, a swimming pool, framed by faint green. Mila must have been crouched in some bushes or something, the foliage blurred out and the distant scene in clear view.

Another cycle of several photos, another record of a blow. I'd had enough by the time the stills showed Willow fall to the tile surround of the idyllic pool deck and handed the phone to Crew. I met the star's eyes as I did. And while I felt horrible for her, I did my best to hide my pity. Because she was waiting for it, I could see that on her face. The stillness that had descended, the tight expectation of judgment.

"He changed," she said, normally vibrant and kind voice dulled out by her pain. "After this last concussion. I think it did permanent damage."

"He's always been abusive, Willow," Mila said. Chided, really.

Willow's face snapped to anger. "Not to me."

"So that made it okay?" The woman beside me vibrated with a surge of her own fury. "It didn't."

Willow sagged back again, the moment of heat she'd managed to stir gone, leaving her a rag doll of broken hopes. "It wasn't supposed to be this way."

"The injury," I said, knowing what she was going to say before I asked the question. "To your back. It wasn't from the stunt, was it?"

She didn't comment vocally, but her faint nod answered my question. The damage to her person was from Skip. And I was suddenly in Mila's camp. Kind of glad the jerk was dead. A horrible place to find myself, really. Still.

Justice could be a killer.

"I tried so hard to convince her to go to the police." Mila's crying had ceased but her fanaticism was alive and well. "I sent her copies of the photos, told her I'd go with her."

"Skip found them," Willow said, a faintly accusing tone in her voice. "He hit me because of them."

Mila shrugged. "You knew what he was." No sympathy.

Wow. What a hideous scab we'd just jerked free from the woman's wound. I had to sit back a moment, my stomach churning for the two women, one a stalker with the best intentions, the other an abused wife and star no one would ever suspect had anything but a perfect life. And a dead football hero who was a monster between them.

I instantly imagined these two plotting his death, creating this entire scene for our benefit, to displace guilt back and forth so neither could be convicted with 100% reasonable doubt. Willow was, after all, an excellent actress. And for a woman who loved her that deeply, Mila surely could pull off a stellar performance.

Crew's mind, it appeared, was hurtling down the same road, and from my father's deep frown so was his, so at least I wasn't alone.

"Ms. Pink," the sheriff said in a soft and understanding voice. "Why didn't you leave him?"

She shot to her feet, Willow's pale face sunken and hollow, eyes narrowed, lips thinned. She no longer looked the stunning star and instead appeared to me a frail and shadowed wraith of a woman, the dregs of who she used to be.

"That," she said, "Sheriff, is none of your business." And before anyone could stop her, she stalked from the room and retreated upstairs.

CHAPTER TWENTY-THREE

I T WAS ONLY MOMENTS later when Julian and Stella, obviously ignoring Crew's orders to stay out of the way, stomped into the sitting room while Mila shrank beside me, huddling in fear as they confronted the sheriff. I found it very interesting my dad hung back, arms crossed, eyes narrowed as he simply observed how Crew handled this new challenge without offering any kind of support.

It had to be hard for my father to just stand by after decades as a deputy and then a sheriff himself. I knew I was having difficulty keeping my mouth shut while Willow's agent and director both started shouting at once.

Crew finally held up both hands, his face locked in a firm yet understanding expression I wouldn't have been able to maintain, so kudos for that. "If you'll speak one at a time," he said, "I'll be happy to answer your questions."

Somehow he reached them, despite the quietness of his voice. Only then did I realize he'd mastered my father's technique, that near-mystical and powerful ability to use sheer influence and will to silence those who were in the deep throws of emotion. I'd watched Dad do it over the years and always felt in awe of that skill. Now that I saw Crew could do it too, I wondered just how hard it might be to figure out for myself.

Interesting and altogether not the point at the moment. And yet, there it was.

"How dare you attack Willow like that?" So this was how the conversation was going to go? I'd had enough already and stood, creeping around them, leaving Mila on the sofa. Dad joined her while she watched me leave with a mournful expression, my pug on my heels. I exhaled in relief as the pounding questioning went on, more indignant and angry than helpful.

Let Crew deal with those two. I had someone I needed to talk to before she recovered from the reveal of what her life was really like.

She wasn't in her room and, when I returned downstairs and peeked in the kitchen, I found her making tea. Carter stood off in one corner, nodding to me and I nodded back, happy to see he was watching over her. She didn't even seem to notice him, and I suppose I understood that was also her reality.

"Willow." I took the box of tea bags from her hand and seated her gently on the stool, waited for her to hug her wrap around her before pouring her tea. She didn't say a word, her face quiet and reposed, but the vulnerable feeling to her hadn't gone away. If anything she was even more exposed and frail than she had been, as if Mila's accusation and proof had torn away everything that kept her together.

I set the cup and saucer in front of her, pulling up a stool next to her, Petunia whining softly before scooting up close enough she could lean against Willow's legs. She smiled down at the pug and scratched the top of her head before a soft sob escaped her. She covered her face in both hands, weeping into them a long moment while I just sat there and let her be.

I caught sight of Carter as he silently left, eyes meeting mine a moment before he was gone. So he trusted me to watch over her, nice to know. And was uncomfortable enough being in the know he chose to give her privacy.

When this was over, I really had to have a long and hard look at how I felt about Carter Melnick.

Willow looked up at last, accepting the paper napkin I liberated from the stack near the spice rack, delicately blowing her nose before sighing out a shaking breath. "Thank you, Fee," she said, crumpling it in her hand and clinging to it like it meant something to her. "I'm so sorry this is happening to you."

And that, I think, was the cusp of Willow Pink. The heart in her, so big and caring, so there for others and herself last, had to be the real reason she stayed. I wanted to shake her suddenly, to make her mad or laugh or anything but this depth of grief and guilt that she was the one who'd done wrong.

She looked up into my eyes, hers clearer and more controlled than I expected. "He asked me why I stayed," she said. Sniffled. Shrugged. "I loved Skip,

Fee. From day one, the moment we met in elementary school. We've been together forever." Willow sipped her tea, set it aside as if she wasn't even sure why she had it in front of her. "I know he wasn't a good person to others. I carry that guilt with me. Did my best to protect the ones he tried to hurt. But he was always good to me. Always."

"Until." I leaned in, elbows on the counter, keeping all pity from my voice, my face. "Last year."

"This last injury changed him like nothing else ever did." She tossed her head back, hair flying over her shoulders, her steel core showing at last, though her weariness matched my own. A kind of acceptance settled around her like her long, dark hair, a resignation that made me sad. "I couldn't believe it, the first time he hit me. I've seen him angry. Jealous. I've seen him so worked up about his career and fearful of being replaced he's ruined other players. Gotten them fired. While I did nothing, buried myself in my work and accepted that was who he was with other people. Until he hit me that night in Las Vegas. And everything changed."

"Did you tell anyone?" Again my inner redhead raged, that he'd have been dead, dismembered and disposed of permanently within five seconds of hitting me. But would he? If I was in her situation, would I do what I thought I would or what she did?

"No," she said, staring at her hands clasped on the counter in front of her. "I had no idea Mila had taken those photos. But honestly, it's not like we were alone. There were three bodyguards there that night. And not one of them stopped him." While she might not have sounded angry about that, I had to clench my jaw against the need to go find Carter and kick him where it would hurt so much he'd never, ever father children. Or walk again. Though, I had no proof he'd been there. Didn't matter just then. Not even a little bit.

Willow sighed again, even managed to smile, like she'd made it past the worst and was emerging from the dark blossom of her grief and guilt. "He wasn't getting any younger," she said. "Neither am I. But while my career as a leading actress has a shelf life, I at least could keep working as long as I was careful about my choices. Once Skip was done, he was done."

"You knew he was taking too many painkillers." That much was obvious.

"I talked him into trying the Quexol," she said. "The doctors said it might take the edge off the injury, maybe help him come back to me. But it made him ill and slow and the team noticed. So he stopped taking it."

"And hit you again?" So hard to say in such a non-judging tone. I managed. Barely.

"Yes, twice. But the worst was the day he found the photos Mila sent." She shook like a tremor took her then settled. Memory was a powerful thing and she had to be reliving the experience. So vivid it rocked her in her seat. "That day, at the pool. He kicked me when I was down, fractured two vertebra before the bodyguards could pull him off me."

At least they did something. "Matt and Evelyn," I said. "Did they know?"

She laughed, startling me. "Those two," she said, a spark of anger in her eyes telling me she'd be okay. "They kept shoveling drugs into him and telling him he was a star. Pushing him to play when he needed to retire. Needed to quit before it killed him." Her voice caught, a hitch at the word kill, and in that instant I knew she was innocent. Not because of proof or an alibi or anything else. Just instinct.

But could I trust my instincts when it came to protecting a battered woman from being punished for possibly murdering her abuser?

"I even caught him stealing mine," she went on, unaware of the battle going on in my head. "I don't know for sure, but I think he was up to thirty pills a day." That couldn't be good. "Regular dose is five to six, Fee."

Okay then.

"I even stood there and watched him down fifteen in one dose." She shook her head, as if unable to believe what she'd just said. "Right before his last game."

"How many did he take today?" Well, yesterday. It was almost 1AM. Why was I still up? A wave of weariness made me dizzy as she answered.

"I don't know for sure," she said. "And it doesn't matter, does it? Everyone knew he was taking them. That he was overtaking them. It would take a massive dose of something stronger to make him OD."

"The Quexol," I said. "Crew already confirmed that." But I felt better knowing that bit of information was wrapped up. "Willow," I said, "this is a hard question. But who would you choose if you had to? Who do you think killed Skip?"

She didn't comment a long moment, luminous eyes locked on mine. And then she twitched, like she'd come to some decision and trusted me with the result.

"Matt," she whispered. "He was about to lose his job because Skip reported him to the association for pushing drugs on football players." Her lower lip trembled. "And he was going to fire Evelyn because his contract didn't get renewed. He was done and he knew it."

That was a bombshell. "You're sure he wasn't getting signed back?"

"It wasn't official," she said. "But I'm positive he was done. And I also know Skip was determined to take them both down with him when he crashed and burned."

CHAPTER TWENTY-FOUR

I LEFT WILLOW IN her room a short time later, hoping she'd get some rest and wondering if I was going to be able to do the same soon. I took a long moment at the top of the stairs, the quiet of the house telling me everyone who was into shouting and tossing accusations had either stopped or gone to bed, too. The soft ticking of the grandfather clock offered a bit of a soothing backdrop as I finally sighed out my weariness and headed down the stairs.

I found Dad and Crew talking quietly in the sitting room, Mom with them. Petunia left me to leap up on the sofa next to my mother and snort a deep exhale of her own before settling her chin on Mom's

p and closing her eyes. Poor pug, she was as tired as
I felt.

"Jill and Robert took Mila Martin to the office,"
Crew said as I settled beside Mom. And realized if I
didn't get up shortly I'd be spending what was left of
the night here in this soft and welcoming cushiony
deliciousness. "I'm hoping seeing her led away in
cuffs will distract the press long enough to give us
breathing room.

Glaring lights on the other side of the sitting
room windows told me the media weren't going
anywhere soon. Funny how I'd gotten used to them
out there already. And what an oasis of quiet
Petunia's felt like just now.

I filled them in on what Willow told me and,
when I was done, Mom slipped her arm around my
shoulders and hugged me to her.

"That poor, poor girl," she said. "But I'm with
Fee. I don't think Willow killed her husband."

"Or Mila," Dad said, surprising me when he
spoke. He hadn't said much the last little while. Crew
seemed to agree, nodding.

"She might have wanted him dead, but she wasn't
in a position to deliver the dose. So that leaves us
with those closest to him."

"I vote we all go to bed and let our minds rest." Mom stood, the pug groaning her unhappiness with the loss of her pillow. "Fee, Dad and I are taking the Blue Suite in the carriage house so we can keep an eye on the yard and that fence, all right?"

"I didn't get a chance to clean it." Guilt over that was stronger than I expected. I was slacking at my job, the one thing I really seemed to enjoy these days.

"Already taken care of," she said with a smile.

"Thanks, Mom. Night." I watched them go, sinking deeper into the sofa, smiling a bit at the sight of Dad holding my mother's hand as they waved and departed. Startled when Crew sat next to me, Petunia now between us as she scooted over to make me her new head rest.

"I'm sorry," he said, so softly I almost didn't think he spoke until he forged on. "About the sandwich comment."

Oh, that. "Crew," I said. But he cut me off, shook his head.

"I'm hard on you," he said. "Hard on myself." So hesitant, so still. I held my breath as he spoke again in jerky sentences that sounded like he struggled to speak them. "You're good at this. All of it." His hand rose, waved into the air in a vague gesture I understood anyway. "You make me crazy. But you make me a better cop."

Wow. That was. *Wow.*

He rubbed his eyes, clearly tired, too, and maybe saying things he wouldn't normally. But I was okay with that. "You impress me, Fiona Fleming." He smiled then, the kind of smile I'd wondered if he was capable of. That reached his eyes and lit the middle of him like he was some kind of superhero. "You think differently. Than John. Than me. And I like that about you."

"Thanks." Oh my god, did I just say that? Just that?

But Crew nodded, stood slowly, stretched out that tall drink of water that was his wide shouldered and narrow hipped body before offering his hand. "Bed?"

That word hovered between us for a long, long time while heat rushed to my cheeks and his own turned pink, the kind of deer in the headlights look that washed over his expression so hilarious I burst in to an uncontrollable half-snort, half donkey bray that triggered a shaky laugh of his own.

"I meant," he said. Stopped like he wasn't sure what else to say.

"I know." I took his hand and let him pull me upright. Was still blushing and a bit giggly when I grinned up at him. "Have a good sleep, Sheriff."

I headed for my apartment, the sound of his boots climbing the stairs to the second floor, and felt a shiver. Maybe if I wasn't so tired I would have reacted differently. But to be honest, I was just as pleased with the result.

Crew Turner was impressed by me. I'd take it.

My expectation when I reached my apartment was a two second shedding of shoes and bra before falling on my bed and passing out cold. I wasn't planning to encounter my best friend sitting in the half dark of my living room, waiting for me. Daisy looked like she'd been crying and, though I fought weariness and a moment of selfish irritation, I went right to her and sat next to her, hugging her while she embraced me back.

She'd have done the same for me. Good friend, Fee.

Petunia hopped up and settled right in Daisy's lap and when she released me, she immediately hugged the pug in turn.

"I'm sorry," Daisy whispered. "I should have just went home. No one needs me anyway."

"I need you." I did, too. Despite my desire to sleep it was so nice just to sit there next to her and not think about the horror story unfolding around me.

She tried a smile, sniffled. "You have so much on your plate. I'm the last thing you need." She blubbered a second, my beautiful friend utterly lost. "I thought this might be the right thing for me, Fee. But I'm terrible at it. I spent the whole day trying to fix mistakes I made, from damaging equipment I moved to getting in the way and ruining sound." Wait, the crew was working despite Skip's death? Wow, that was Hollywood, I suppose. "They had to reshoot an entire sequence at French's because I was in the shot." Daisy burst into tears. "And then all this with Willow and Skip and I couldn't even be here to help you and do that much right."

"You were here, helping Mom." That attempt to make her feel better blew up in my face as she wailed briefly before speaking in a hiccupping stutter.

"I was picking up food for the crew," she said. "And I got that all wrong, too. I gave them all meat and they're vegans." She buried her face in Petunia's fur. "I'm a loser, Fee. I'm a total loser."

I hugged her again and rocked her a little, knowing she just needed a good cry and a shoulder to do it on. When she was done, she wiped at her nose with the sleeve of her plaid shirt and did manage a little smile.

"What am I going to do?" She sounded so small and broken and it wasn't fair. She was the best, the coolest, the most amazing person I knew. No way was life getting Daisy Bruce down. Not if I had anything to say about it.

"You," I said, "are going to get some sleep. And then tomorrow, you're going to try again. Because the Daisy I know isn't a loser or a quitter or stupid. She's awesome and they are lucky to have her."

She shrugged. "Maybe I should come back to Petunia's?" She said it like a question, hopeful. "I love it here, Fee. It's the only place I've been happy in a long time."

I wanted to say yes. More than anything, nothing would have made me more overjoyed. "Daisy," I said instead, "there will come a day you and I are the two crazy old ladies who run this place, who drink too much gin out of teacups and yell at cute boys from the verandah while we cheat at poker." She laughed. Good, perfect. "But I don't want you to settle. You need to keep looking. Because what you want, who you want to be, it might still be out there. And, as much as I hate to think so, you might even need to look outside the borders of Reading to find it."

Saying that almost made me cry. I'd only just found her again after ten years away myself. But I'd had the chance to live life in the real world that had nothing to do with the small town Twilight Zone that was our home. And she deserved that same chance.

Daisy seemed shocked by the suggestion but nodded. "Okay, Fee," she said. "I'll be brave, like you, as much as I can."

"And when and if you're ready," I said, "you come back to Petunia's if that's what you decide you want."

She hugged me again, sighed out her hurt. Another hug later, she let me go to bed, pulling a quilt over herself while she settled in on my couch, my pug staying with her as if sensing Daisy needed the love while I collapsed and hoped tomorrow might actually be a better day.

CHAPTER TWENTY-FIVE

ONE OF THE CRAPPY parts about the Jones sisters leaving me in the lurch was I had to deal with all the rooms myself. No way was I neglecting that bit of business, not after my own mother had to clean the suite she and Dad used last night. So what if a guy died on me yesterday? I was such a slacker.

Regardless of my determination to keep things as normal as possible, when I woke at six like I normally did, with maybe four and a bit hours sleep under my belt, I sighed out my irritation that along with helping to solve a murder, I had toilets to scrub.

Damn it.

With the rest of the house still asleep—Daisy on the sofa included—I showered quickly and headed upstairs, Petunia following me, doing her business in quick time outside in the garden so she could get to her food bowl as fast as possible. I hefted the bucket and gloves, mop in hand, and hoofed my way to the third floor. Two doors stood open, only the third occupied, the bathroom at the end of the hall my goal. And while cleaning that space might have seemed an odd thing to do in the middle of a murder investigation, Petunia's was my place and there was no way I was letting things slide, even at a time like this.

There was a zen kind of peace that came from scrubbing, I'd discovered, a chance to do lots of thinking and processing and percolation that could lead to ah-ha moments. And so, with determination and cleanliness in mind, I set to sorting out the mess that the single person on this floor left behind.

I recognized the shade of lipstick and the scent of perfume on the towels as Evelyn. The woman was a walking disaster, leaving trash and powder trails and toothpaste blobs everywhere, not to mention the globs of fake blonde hair clumped in the tub/shower drain. So gross. I finally finished cleaning what she'd left behind with the satisfaction that comes from a job well done, the sound of birds outside reminding me it was spring, sunshine casting sparkling beams through the window.

The trash can nearly filled the small plastic bag I brought to dump it in, but as I tipped it to empty it, the corner slipped and something hard and small escaped. The bottle bounced on the tile and rolled to a halt at the foot of the claw tub, on its side. My heart skipping, I crouched over it, tilting my head to read the label. Someone had blacked it out with a marker, but I could just make out the raised lettering under it in the sparkling light of the direct sunbeam.

Quexol.

I stood carefully and washed my rubber gloves, hands shaking, before drying them carefully on a towel. I should have left the evidence collection to Crew, but I couldn't run the risk of leaving this here for someone to stumble on—like the murderer, for example.

A second plastic bag became that bottle's home. I stared down into the full one for a long moment before diving into it with my gloves still on and, in short order, was carefully removing a small syringe from the depths of dirty tissues and plastic wrap, a drop of clear fluid still inside.

That followed the bottle into the bag. As soon as I finished tying it off I sank to the toilet and sat with my face in my hands, breathing steadily to keep the dizziness at bay.

Had I just found the murder weapon in Evelyn's bathroom?

It was hard to slowly walk the hall to the stairs, to pause and listen at her door without barging in and accusing her of killing Skip. To calmly descend two stories to the foyer with the trash and my cleaning kit in one hand and the evidence in the other.

I was pretty proud of myself, actually, when I spotted Dad and Crew in the sitting room and didn't run the last few steps, instead with a professional and detached air handing the sheriff the clear bag with the syringe and bottle like I knew what I was doing.

"Third floor bathroom trash," I said. "Evelyn's the only one on that level."

Crew's eyes widened, eyebrows shooting up while Dad whistled low.

"Nice catch, kid," my father said.

"Now, if you'll excuse me," I said, turning my back on them, "I have more toilets to scrub."

I have no idea what they thought of that particular pronouncement and nor did I care. But instead of going back upstairs, I went to the kitchen. Because after that little performance I really, really needed coffee.

I guess I shouldn't have been surprised to find Pamela sitting at the counter, waiting for me, Mom serving her a hot cup herself while the newspaper woman waved and smiled and Mom gestured at me with the pot.

No use arguing that we were supposed to keep Pamela out. Instead, too tired and wound up to argue, I accepted a brimming mug with the perfect amount of cream and sugar and gulped my first mouthful of the hot liquid despite the temperature.

Petunia stared at her bowl in mournful silence until Mom dumped a handful of diced pineapple in it. Our conversation proceeded to the snuffle and snorting sound of the pug devouring her sugary treat.

"You look like you saw a ghost, Fee." Mom paused her watermelon chopping and waited for me to answer.

I told them both what I'd found and screw the consequences. Of course, by the time I was done the sound of shouting out in the foyer reached through the kitchen door so it wasn't like Pamela wasn't going to get the full scoop anyway as the three of us, Petunia trailing after me, pushed open the door and watched Evelyn lose her crap all over Crew.

Oddly, Stella had joined her and the two were arguing at the volume and ferocity that made it impossible to make out full sentences. This time Crew's skill at silencing them wasn't working, the pair of powerful women cornering him against the staircase as if they were going to skin him alive any second now.

Dad stood off to one side, a faint grin on his face, but when I met his gaze he wiped it clean and I realized then how much he was enjoying this entire mess. Hadn't he said so at the lodge when Crew had recruited both of us to help him investigate the death of Mason Patterson? That not having to be responsible for the outcome was refreshing to him. And clearly my father hadn't changed his mind in that regard. Maybe just being involved was enough to keep him gleefully engaged and any desire he had to take over drowned out by the utter delight of watching someone else deal with what he had to manage for so long.

Stella's voice finally won over Evelyn's and I made out her last statement before they both fell silent between breaths. "You can't keep us here any longer!"

"Willow did not kill her husband," Evelyn snarled. "And the fact you're accusing me now tells me your Podunk, small town redneck county sheriff routine is frighteningly authentic." She crossed her arms over her chest. "Where are the real police to handle this?"

Even I winced at that blow. But Crew kept it together.

"If you would answer my questions, Ms. Prichard, instead of shouting at me and pretending to be offended, maybe we could sort this out faster. But," his voice dropped to a threatening growl, "I can tell you right now, this Podunk redneck sheriff will pin your ass to the ground if he finds out you murdered Skip Anderson."

That backed them both off.

"Sheriff," Stella said, sounding mollified and a bit chastised, "it's just unbelievable you could think any of us had anything to do with his death."

"The lack of security around here," Evelyn said, not in retreat like her counterpart, but at least no longer shouting, "means anyone could have had access to that bathroom. And planted that evidence against me."

"I'm well aware of that," Crew said. "But you have questions to answer to before I can make that determination. And fingerprints to be lifted to prove your innocence. Or your guilt."

"And the second I'm proved innocent," Evelyn snapped, back into full-on fury, "I'll be suing you and this little crap hole town for false arrest!"

"Ma'am," Crew said, "you're not under arrest."

"But I'm not free to go, so what does that tell me, Sheriff?"

She kind of had a point. But no one got to confirm that, not when Olivia suddenly burst through the front door, slamming it shut behind her, the sound of the gathered news media shouting at her for her attention barely muffled by the heavy wood.

"I understand," she said, dark eyes narrowed, fully pulled together since yesterday's meltdown, at least on the surface, "some evidence in the case has been found and a suspect is in custody?"

Crew hesitated. "Sort of," he said. And winced.

I wouldn't have wanted to be him at that moment while she pushed off from the door and stormed over to get in his face, but with the low and dangerous threatening that neither of the other two women tried on him.

"Sheriff Turner," she said in a hissing growl, "I have been patient. But you are not only holding a famous star prisoner here, you are creating a slew of opportunities for our town to be threatened with lawsuits."

Evelyn looked nastily pleased. So her little threat wasn't a threat. She'd already been talking to a lawyer? Whoops.

"That is why," Olivia turned away from Crew and addressed Evelyn and Stella, "I've made the decision to call in state police to help with this investigation." Oh boy. They could poke their noses in if they wanted, but likely held off out of respect for Crew. Still, I bet they'd just been chomping at the bit to get their hands on this case. That had to be an ego blow for Crew. Though a private part of me—selfish to the core—wondered if it might be better if they did come take this off my hands and let life go back to normal.

Fee. Shame on you.

Bad vibes pay off, typically, and this time was no exception. Crew chose that moment to glance my way and spotted Pamela standing between me and Mom. Just before his already tense expression turned to flat out hell no. And, of course, at the exact same instant, Olivia chose to look our way, too, didn't she?

Before either of them could lose their crap all over my foyer, however, Mom took a firm and decisive step forward and held up one hand for attention. Surprisingly, both the sheriff and the mayor closed their half opened mouths and listened as Mom spoke.

"Pamela is one of us," she said. "And I would rather she reported the truth than those vultures out there churning up rumors and guesses while making Reading look bad."

Both hesitated while Pamela spoke up.

"As it happens, Sheriff," she said in a mild mannered tone that almost sounded amused. At Mom's little show? Or this whole situation? "I have some information for you that might be helpful."

Crew grunted something that might have been impolite but I didn't catch it so I chose to think otherwise. Willow descended the staircase with Julian on her heels, Matt trailing after them while the sheriff gestured for Pamela to join him in the sitting room.

I motioned for Willow to join me but Olivia was already grasping her hand, gushing all over her.

"My deepest apologies for the accusations and the inconveniences of this horrible, horrible affair." She was in full on politician mode and missed, in her enthusiasm, Willow's mask descend in response. But I saw it settle, the way she went from real person to persona in a practiced moment. And that made me wonder all over again. Great actress, abusive spouse.

Damn it. She had the motive and opportunity. Did she plant that bottle and syringe in the third floor bathroom?

My speculation ended as Pamela exited the sitting room, heading past us with a shrug for me and a wink for Mom, disappearing into the kitchen and, I assumed, out to the hole in the fence that I had to make my priority today. Crew came to a serious halt in the center of the foyer, his attention focused on Willow in a way that brought Olivia's next extravagant apology to a stuttering halt.

"Ms. Pink," Crew said in that soft and questioning tone that told me she was his prime suspect, "why didn't you tell me you'd filed for divorce?"

CHAPTER TWENTY-SIX

WHY DID I FEEL betrayed? She never told me, despite ample opportunities. Not that she owed me any kind of explanation or even the time of day. But I had this weird impression she liked me, that we were kind of friends already. And friends told each other things like this, right?

Willow's face settled into flat emptiness as she replied.

"I knew how it would look," she said, holding Crew's gaze and not looking in my direction at all. On purpose? Was she feeling guilty? "Besides, the divorce has nothing to do with it. I loved Skip, but he wasn't the man I married. So you tell me, Sheriff.

Why murder him if I planned on divorcing him anyway?"

"I can think of one thing in particular," Crew said. "Times millions."

She snorted, looked away at last, but her expression didn't soften. "We had a prenup. Skip insisted. He was first draft pick before I ever went to L.A. and he had his millions before mine made a debut. Divorce meant neither of us got a cent of each other's money."

"But his death makes you beneficiary, I take it?" Crew didn't sound convinced of his own line of questioning.

"Seriously, Sheriff," Stella snapped. "Willow Pink is worth far more than Skip Anderson could ever hope to be and her star is still burning brightly. Why would she need to murder a failing football hero for his money? Ridiculous."

I had to agree. And with the divorce in the works, killing him made no sense. Unless it was a crime of passion, a heat of the moment thing. Except filling a syringe and injecting it at a time she knew he was pretty close to overdosing on his own? That sounded like premeditation to me. But no, if he was that near the edge, why not just sweet talk him into taking enough to do the job? Why risk getting caught by doing it herself?

Questions and more questions.

"Did Skip know about the divorce?" I spoke up before I could stop myself and despite the softness of my tone everyone fell silent and turned to me, even Crew.

Willow nodded slowly. "He knew," she said. "And he agreed not to fight me on it. So you see, Sheriff Turner, I have no motive whatsoever to kill the man I used to love." She barked out a little laugh that made Petunia whine softly in response. "I was planning to accept my failure and the shame of my marriage's end and walk away." She spun, truly angry now, or so it seemed to me, storming halfway up the stairs before pausing to glare down at Crew. "If you'll excuse me, I'm going to lie down."

No one said anything, the gathering scattering instead, returning to their rooms or passing me and entering the dining room where Mom hurriedly began delivering food. Daisy had appeared when I wasn't paying attention and helped her, keeping her head down and throwing me shy smiles but not speaking, either.

Great, a silent house. Just what I needed.

I turned to go back to the kitchen with Petunia when Matt almost bumped into me, our trajectories on course for impact. I squeaked then stopped as he smiled his apology, dark eyes still sad.

"Matt," I said, "Willow told me about the accusations Skip made against you to the league." Because preamble wasn't on my menu of options this morning.

His face darkened and he choked a moment before he managed to inhale. But rather than yell at me he nodded. "It doesn't matter now," he said. "I'm so tired of all of it. Of Skip and trying to protect him while he spiraled out of control. That boy owed a lot of people for keeping him afloat and he paid us back by trying to destroy us."

"You and Evelyn," I said.

Matt sighed. "Yes." His attitude shifted while he relaxed somewhat as if getting it out there made things better. "Truth is, every coach has access to painkillers, Fee. It's common practice to load up your players. These guys, they think they're invincible, act like gladiators or something. And heaven forbid they show weakness or injury or miss a game. The competition for the starting lineup is so fierce any flicker of failure can be a death sentence." He flinched at his choice of words. "Career wise, I mean."

"So you were just doing your job." I wasn't in a position to judge him, but I did anyway.

"What else do you do with guys who think they need to laugh in the face of pain to be a hero?" He looked angry suddenly. "I was one of them, once upon a time, but I never made it past college ball. I never felt the pressure Skip did until I was standing beside him while he downed a handful of pills because his head hurt so bad he could barely stand. And I let him go out there, over and over again. I did what the team doctors told me to do and I'm ashamed to admit it. But I was scared for my job."

"And yet he was turning you in for over plying him with painkillers." Weird. But if his concussion was that bad, maybe Skip wasn't thinking straight? Matt seemed confused by my statement, anger fading. "That had nothing to do with it," he said. "According to the complaint I received, I was under investigation because one of the kids Skip got kicked off the team committed suicide. And I was named in his goodbye world note."

Huh. "Was Skip, too?"

Matt nodded, grim. "Bad press for him was a different thing all together, though. He could brush it off as competitiveness or sour grapes. But me? A minor coach brought on by the team star? Especially since I was named in a wrongful death suit by the family."

I wondered if Pamela knew about that.

"The team got it suppressed," he said, sounding sad at last. "Jason Hagan. That poor kid. I knew Skip was riding him, but I had no idea it was that bad. Until he was canned. And Skip laughed about it. When I heard Jason had offed himself, that was the first time I really hated the guy I used to idolize."

I didn't know what to say to that.

"I had no reason to kill Skip," Matt said at last, hands in his pockets, face dark with sorrow. "My career was over, regardless. And so was his. He didn't get offered a new contract this year. So the writing was on the wall for all of us."

"Including Evelyn," I said.

Matt nodded, though reluctantly. "She didn't do it, either." That was a bit hasty and without conviction.

"Thanks, Matt," I said. "Go have breakfast. It'll all be over soon."

I left him to enter the dining room on his own, aiming for the kitchen, hoping I was right but more confused by this entire mess than ever.

CHAPTER TWENTY-SEVEN

I EXPECTED CREW TO be interrogating Evelyn, not to find that she'd snuck past me and into the kitchen, accepting a large cup of coffee from Mom with an eager look on her face.

"You make the best java I've had in years, Lucy," she gushed to my mother, inhaling from the massive mug steaming under her nose. "I should steal you and take you back to L.A. with me."

"You'll have to fight me for her," I said, joining them and taking a fresh cup myself.

Evelyn sank to a stool as if invited, eyes locked on me. I'd judged her from the moment I laid eyes on her as hard edged and pushy, and with good reason. But the woman behind that gaze seemed much more human to me now and instead of letting the opportunity pass me by, I sat with her as Daisy bustled into the kitchen and took plates from Mom before hurrying out again.

I guess Carter was busy guarding Willow. Oh well.

"Matt was telling you about the lawsuit, wasn't he?" She didn't beat around bushes. Evelyn tipped her mug twice and swallowed with gusto before speaking again. "You do know it's all bull?"

"So Skip didn't bully some kid off the team and that same kid didn't kill himself and name Matt and Skip in the suicide note?" She wanted blunt? I could do blunt.

Mom hissed softly, turning to stare at me in angry shock while Evelyn shook her head.

"Of course, that part happened," she said. "But the suit is crap." Okay, if she said so. "It's a tough business, not for the weak at heart. Those guys are giants in their own minds and if anyone tries to bring them down or shove them aside they take action. And that's what Skip did."

"Jason Hagan was challenging him?" Well, Willow did say Skip was aging out and from the sound of the lack of contract he was done with the team he'd just played for at least.

Evelyn nodded with vigor, her coffee sloshing as she did. "It was all Skip, I promise you that," she said. "Matt might have turned a blind eye, certainly. So did all the coaches. But he was a bastard, that Skipper of ours. A real mean streak to him, concussion or not. I think the injury to his brain just brought out the real him rather than causing it."

"You still repped him." Not judging. Not. Judging.

She shrugged and made a wry face that brought out the wrinkles around her thin lips. "It's the business, kiddo. He was a dick, but he could play football. And those boys aren't paid to be nice."

Right. She was totally right. And I needed to shake off this growing anger inside me if I was going to ask the questions I needed to ask without setting the wrong tone.

"So, this kid who died," I said. "Who was he?"

"Just another wanna be," Evelyn said. "Only he actually had what it took. Or I thought he did. Showed real promise. I almost approached Jason, would have if Skip hadn't taken his talent as a personal affront and did his best to ruin the kid first." She gulped some coffee, gaze in the distant past. "I'd seen him jealous before, but this was beyond. It was all Skip talked about. How Jason did this wrong and Jason couldn't throw right, endlessly, on and on. Broken record stuff. And a sign he was cracking, in my opinion."

How practical of her. "But you stayed with him?"

"What can I say," she shrugged. "I'm a sucker for a paycheck." At least she was honest about her job and her motives. That I could at least respect, if not what she actually did.

"So how did Skip get him booted?" She was being so forthcoming I wanted to keep her talking. Mom topped up her mug without a word and a nod for me while Evelyn seemed absorbed in the past again.

"Jason got a chance at starting lineup," she said. "Announced at practice before game night. Skip's place, no less. I thought his head would explode. Instead, that day, he hit the kid over and over again. Legally, totally inside the rules. But hard and relentless, you know? The last one was an utter train wreck. I've never seen anyone get laid out that hard and not get injured."

"He purposely hurt his own teammate," I said, knowing the shock and disbelief in my voice had to be heavy.

She nodded though, didn't seem surprised by my reaction. "Not just once, not by accident. He systematically took that kid down until he couldn't fight back then snapped him like a twig."

Holy crap.

"Oh, best part though," Evelyn said like none of this was a big deal in the long run of her career, "was the aftermath, right? Coaches are full of praise, put Skip back on the lineup because he made such a great example of what to avoid and what not to do on the field, like he'd done Jason a favor." How disgusting was that? "Then Skip does the best buddy routine, takes the kid under his wing. And makes sure to push him so far into painkillers Jason can't walk straight let alone catch a football. Ruined him while being an exemplary part of the team."

My disgust for Skip Anderson ratcheted up about as high as it could have gone and then some, my stomach turning as I thought about purposely ruining someone like that all out of jealousy and utter evil.

"Kid lasted about a month after the accident," Evelyn said. Winced at her choice of words and I wondered if that's what everyone chose to call Skip's attack to make themselves feel better about not doing anything to stop it. "And while I get that maybe Jason might not have been tough enough, if the kid had been allowed to evolve I know he'd have been a star. Instead, Skip let him tie his own noose and hang himself with it. And laughed about it when Jason got canned. To his face. So the kid would know just who set him up to crash and burn."

"You know," Mom interrupted, voice mild—a warning like I'd never heard from her before, that sweetly level tone—"that kind of person might find themselves murdered for what they'd done."

My mother was a genius.

And Evelyn seemed to agree. "You got it, Lu," she said as if they were old friends. "If Jason was still alive, he'd be my prime suspect. But he's been dead about six months. And the family settled not so long ago, for a crap ton of cash to shut them up."

Didn't mean it was over in their eyes, though, did it? "And your second choice?"

Evelyn looked uncomfortable. "Willow," she finally whispered. "Damn that girl, she looks soft and sweet but she's got a backbone like an iron bar and enough venom saved up to do it. I'm sure of it."

"You defended her earlier," I said.

Evelyn winced, downed her coffee, set the mug on the counter. "I did," she said. "It's my job. With Skip dead, the sheriff was right. She's the beneficiary. Though money was never a motive. How he treated her? We all knew it was happening. And I have to live with the fact I didn't do a thing to stop it."

At last it appeared, the grief, the woman behind the snarky and heavy handed agent. For a moment I was sure she was going to break down and weep. Instead, she jerked herself together and stood, nodding to me, to Mom.

"I didn't kill him," she said. Shrugged. "If I did, I wouldn't be damned stupid enough to leave the evidence where you could find it, I promise you that." I didn't doubt her. "Now, if you'll excuse me, I think I'll have some breakfast and try to figure out what to do now that my meal ticket is gone."

Mom and I stared at each other as she walked to the door, both of our heads turning at once as Evelyn paused and spoke one last time.

"You might want to ask that mayor of yours," she said in a thoughtful voice, "what she was going to do about Skip's decision to renege on his contract with her."

And left before we could scrape our jaws off the floor.

CHAPTER TWENTY-EIGHT

OM RECOVERED FIRST, SPINNING on me with her spatula held out like a weapon. "You bring Olivia Walker here," she snarled, jabbing at the floor with her utensil, "to me. Right now."

And I thought her sweet tone was scary. I scrambled to my feet and hurried toward the door, but I didn't have to drag Olivia to see Mom. She came in all on her own, though I doubted she had any idea the crap storm she was about to face.

If anything, she seemed distracted and took our presence for granted as she slipped her phone into her jacket pocket, the fitted dark gray suit and cream shell she wore making her olive skin seem ghostly.

"Coffee, Lu, please," she said. "I need the energy."

Mom let her sit, handed her a mug, didn't say a word while Olivia rattled on like she was the only person in the room who mattered.

"I'm exhausted," she said. "Fielding requests for interviews and setting up the shooting around Willow's unavailability and dealing with the state troopers. It's been a mess." She finally looked up from her mug and into Mom's tight, quiet face before turning to find me staring at her with my arms crossed over my chest and that same expression plastered in place because I might have been my father's daughter but when push came to shove, the redhead came out. You bet she did.

"Whatever is the matter with the two of you?" She thudded her mug on the counter, trying for offended. But the faint flicker of anxiety that crossed her face told me she knew we knew and she wasn't ready to admit anything just yet.

"You," Mom said in a crisp and undeniable tone, "are going to march your ass," she didn't move, didn't have to, threat hanging between them, "to Crew Turner and tell him everything, Olivia." She paused for effect while the mayor stuttered. "Before the press finds out Skip Anderson was planning to break his contract and this turns against Reading." That got the mayor's attention. "Now his tirade in the parade makes sense," Mom said, finally starting to pace. "He reneged already, didn't he? Set this up all on his own to humiliate our town. And you knew about it."

The mayor didn't comment, just sagged at last and stared into her coffee. "Willow said she'd take care of it."

"Do you realize how bad this looks?" Mom didn't honestly think Olivia killed Skip? Still, it was motive for anyone who knew the mayor and her drive to promote Reading. And keeping it a secret did look bad. The media could twist less into more and ruin everything. "And what an utter mess his disastrous rampage left behind? It's all over the internet, Olivia. Him ranting about Reading. Your plan backfired and if you'd just had the courage to tell someone, we could have tried to keep him out of it. Instead, you buried your head up your ass and let that piece of garbage who no one will want to remember when it comes out he used to beat his stunning star wife demean our town and die on my daughter!"

Whew. Mom was wound up. And I didn't blame her. Everything she said made sense.

Olivia didn't get to respond. Distraction broke our focus, the sudden sound of voices in the back garden, many, many voices, shouting Willow Pink's name. I spun and ran, Petunia on my heels, Olivia right behind me, and out into the spring morning to find the actress cornered against the house by a large pack of reporters who had clearly invaded my privacy.

The bedlam made it hard to focus, the crush of bodies bruising me as I forced my way through them to Willow and got a good grip on her arm. I looked up to find Carter on her other side, struggling to keep the reporters at bay while Willow's face paled out to almost nothing.

And then Crew was there, Jill and Robert, clearing away the crowd with the help of three tall troopers in dark uniforms. I took the break in the action they created and jerked Willow behind me into the kitchen, slamming the door in Olivia's face, Carter leaning against it to protect the star from the surge of reporters still trying to reach her despite the police presence.

"I'm sorry," Willow whispered, clinging to my hand. "I just wanted some air. I didn't realize…" She sobbed then, hugged me. "Why won't they just leave me alone?"

It was so hard not to feel for her so I didn't try. Though, in all honesty, she should have been used to this kind of attention. Then again, she had just lost her husband, so slack would be cut. And, if she killed Skip, well, you know what? Right now at this moment I was in the good for her department ringing up my let me help next time purchases.

The door thudded as the sound diminished. I gestured for Carter to back off which he did reluctantly, to allow Crew and Olivia inside. The sheriff glared at the body guard but considering Carter had been doing his job, there wasn't much he could say.

Instead, he confronted the already wobbly Willow. "What were you thinking?"

She didn't respond, hand trembling in mine.

"Leave her, Crew," I said, knowing he wouldn't thank me for interfering.

"Tell them, Willow," Olivia blurted. "That Skip wasn't going to renege on his contract with Reading." How desperate she sounded.

Crew glared at her in clear surprise. "What?"

"It's all right, I promise I'll fix it." Olivia seemed more wrapped up in her own story than was good for any of us.

The sheriff groaned, rubbed his face with one hand. "You should have told me, Olivia."

Willow whispered something while the two argued. I leaned in to catch what she said, and instead watched with horror as her eyes rolled back into her head and, without another word and with an almost delicate sigh, crumbled to the floor.

CHAPTER TWENTY-NINE

D R. LLOYD ABERSTOCK ACCEPTED the glass of water I handed him. I was just as happy not to be on the receiving end of his kind smile this time and played a supporting role. He held up the drink to Willow's lips, gently prodding her to sip. There was a bluish tinge to her skin, the transparence that made her look so fresh faced on camera just seeming deathly now, her dark hair framing her thin face, normally luminous eyes sunken into dark pits as she accepted a small drink before turning her head away.

"I'll be all right," she whispered, hoarse and sounding tired. "I just need a minute. Please, don't make any more of a fuss than you already have."

"Passing out after stress isn't a small thing, young lady," Dr. Aberstock said. Now that I could appreciate his presence fully, I remembered how much I loved his manner, had always liked visiting him despite knowing when I did it meant a shot or some kind of unpleasant activity. He had that grandfatherly look to him, white hair thinning but still lush, round, rosy cheeks as healthy as anyone half his age and bright blue eyes that seemed to miss nothing. He offered the glass again and she took another sip before smiling at last. "I seem to recall you used to have trouble with such spells if you weren't eating enough."

"I'm not a little girl anymore," she said, though it didn't sound defensive, more softly amused. "And I've been under worse stress than this since you were my doctor." She flushed, two bright, unhealthy points standing out in stark glow on her prominent cheekbones. "That sounded horrible."

Dr. Aberstock patted her hand, leaning back and handing the glass to me again with his own smile. The Green Suite felt quiet and closed, everyone but me and the doctor banned from the room for now. Carter's swiftness meant Willow hadn't made it all the way to the floor, acting faster than I was able.

Considering she went sideways as she crumbled, knocking into me and shoving me off balance, it could have ended with me down there with her instead of her in his arms before she could carry me to the ground.

Willow might have been thin, but she was still dead weight as she collapsed and, thankfully, Carter was close enough to stop both of us from toppling when she went down. He hadn't paused from there, whisking her out of the kitchen and up the stairs and I raced after him, Crew muttering into the phone for the doctor.

That had only been ten minutes ago but my heart was still beating a little too fast, worry for Willow making me hover, breathless and shocky, likely left over from the events of yesterday.

"I'm so sorry for the dramatics," Willow said, sounding a bit stronger. "I have no idea what happened just now. I haven't passed out like that since grade school."

"I'd say you've worn yourself down to the quick." Dr. Aberstock's gentle smile worked its normal wonders. Willow made no effort to fight to sit up or argue as he went on. "The pressure of your husband's tragic passing—my condolences,

Willow—and the flare up of your injury along with the weighty schedule you keep as an actor. Well, let's say I'm not surprised at all it finally took its toll."

She scrunched her nose at him and I realized then she knew him better than I did, and had to remind myself yet again she grew up in Reading too. "Thank you. It's been... a truly terrible twenty-four hours."

"I want you at the hospital in Falls Station," he said. "Just overnight, for observation. No arguing, young lady." She shook her head, biting her lower lip. "I'll call ahead so they can have a private room ready. I'm sure the sheriff will want to make sure there's security so you're not troubled while you rest."

"I could just rest here." But she didn't sound like she believed it and I was with her on that.

"Get out of Petunia's," I blurted, then blushed. "I didn't mean it that way. You're always welcome." Her widened eyes at my statement turned to softening and a nod. "But you need to distance yourself from this, Willow. Even if just for a night and somewhere you can have medical attention. Just in case."

"Thank you both." She sighed, closed her eyes. A bead of moisture formed in the corners and trailed slowly down her temples and into her dark hair. "I think that might be a great idea."

I left the room with Dr. Aberstock, closing the door softly behind me, having to turn and press my back against it to keep Julian from forcing his way past me. But it was the kindly doctor who placed a firm hand on the manager's chest and shook his head, stern grandpa shutting him down.

"She needs time," he said. Nodded to Crew who hovered in the hall, waiting with an anxious expression while Olivia's hands clasped tightly before her, Stella pacing a tight back and forth at the top of the stairs. "I'll have an ambulance take her to Curtis County General for the night."

"No." Julian snapped that denial. "You want to make things worse? Put Willow Pink in an ambulance and make her look weak. Go ahead, do that and I'll sue this entire town for ruining her career."

That was going a bit far, but I didn't see the need for an ambulance either. The hospital in Falls Station was maybe a fifteen minute drive from here. "Why don't we put her in an inconspicuous car and have Carter take her?" The steaming tension in the hall seemed to ease as I spoke while I met Crew's eyes to win him over. "There's no need to turn this into a bigger circus. And if she can get out of here with no one noticing, there's a better chance she can get some actual rest when she gets to the hospital."

Crew's jaw jumped but he nodded. "I'll tell the state troopers to put guards on her door." He turned and left, but paused at the top of the steps, Stella chewing her nails while he spoke. "Jill's going in the car with Carter." And then he was gone, stomping his way to the first floor while Dr. Aberstock beamed at me and hugged me with genuine caring.

"Well done, Fee," he said. "Now, if you'll all excuse me, I have to call admitting."

I was left alone with Julian, Olivia and Stella, and as soon as the doctor was gone the three of them started their chatter all over again.

"If the press gets wind of this, Willow's next contract could be threatened." Julian's face darkened as he spun on Olivia. "This is all your fault, Mayor Walker. We should never have agreed to this ridiculous propaganda plan you've been pushing on Willow the last two years."

"My fault?" Olivia's indignation snapped like a whip. "Willow signed a contract in full understanding of what she was agreeing to, Julian."

"She's been pushing herself too hard," Stella muttered. "It might be good for her to break her contract on her next picture. Take some time off and recover from her injury and now this."

Every single word that left their mouths triggered my anger. Bubbling, boiling and ready to blow, I stood rigid as Stella finished her thought before drawing an audible breath that caught their attention and turned their three faces toward me.

"Maybe," I said softly, because if I went above that volume I'd be shouting in seconds, "if someone in her life had actually given a crap that her husband was beating her, she wouldn't be in this position in the first place."

"That's not fair," Julian spluttered. "She wouldn't let us help."

"I had no idea," Olivia said. Like she had the right to be offended at a time like this.

Stella, at least, had the good grace to appear guilty.

"You all make me sick." I spun and walked away, knowing I should stay and guard the door so they wouldn't bother Willow, but unable to stop myself from leaving. Thankfully, Carter appeared as if by magic, hurrying past me with a grim expression and anger in his eyes as he met mine on the way by. I half turned to see him plant himself in front of Willow's door with his broad shoulders pressed to the wood, hands clasped before him, face a dark mask of stone.

He'd overheard our conversation then, had he? And thought as little as I did of the trio who should have known better.

Then again, as I set foot in the foyer and tried to pull myself together, I had to accept the sobering thought that it wasn't up to others. That Willow had made the choice to stay. But if I knew anything about men and manipulation—hello, Ryan Richards might not have hit me but he controlled our relationship in ways I was only now uncovering—it was this. We stayed even long after we knew in our dying hearts we shouldn't because we believed they were who we deserved.

Twenty minutes later I slipped around the fence into the Munroe property and checked for straggling press who might have escaped the obvious and loud press conference Olivia started up just a moment ago. The distraction tactic seemed to be working, the noisy crowd at the front of Petunia's drawn in to her update report while I turned and waved to Willow and Carter. She wavered as she walked, but Carter was beside her the whole time and it was a short jaunt, really, so I had little doubt she'd be all right.

So weird to be back here. I hadn't set foot on Peggy Munroe's property since the night she tried to kill me. Her already overgrown garden had turned into a brown mass of dead vegetation, a slightly creepy web of interlaced weeds with the path to the house only vaguely apparent.

Jill waved from the far side of the house, dressed in plain clothes, though to me even her regular jeans and jacket did nothing to hide the no-nonsense about her that screamed deputy. Not that it mattered, as long as Olivia did her job and kept the press occupied.

The mayor's luxury sedan had tinted windows, a perfect choice, though a bit obvious to me. Still, as Willow sank into the back seat and sighed while the soft leather enveloped her, I didn't argue.

Carter took shotgun, Jill nodding to me as she drove away, backing slowly out of the Munroe's driveway and turning right, up the hill and away from Petunia's, though I worried the packed line of news vans would make it impossible for her to escape. But Jill's driving skills were more than up to the task and a moment later they were quietly cruising away, unnoticed.

Perfect. Only then did I realize I was alone with the kind of memories I didn't really want to relive that still woke me up sometimes in the middle of the night, with the horrible old lady grinning at me from the other end of a gun barrel.

Time to go home.

I blame my weariness and my focus on Willow's escape for the fact I didn't see Randy Russell sneak up behind me. The scream that escaped me? Yeah, part and package with the aforementioned. Randy actually laughed as I panted, clutching my chest with both hands, my anger roused once again.

"What the hell is wrong with you?" I stomped past him, furious not only had he caught me flatfooted but likely knew Willow had left and would be reporting it despite our best efforts to the contrary. Well, whatever. We'd done our best.

"You didn't call me," he said, tossing that out with a light and teasing tone.

I stopped, spun, feet grinding over dead foliage and stirring the scent of decay and mildew, enough to make me want to sneeze. "You have something to tell me, Mr. Russell? I'm right here. Tell me."

His eyes narrowed as he looked away, hesitant before he shrugged. "Not here," he said. "Too many ears around, more than you know. How about I call you, Red?"

I didn't recall giving him permission to choose a nickname for me, especially one so generic. "Whatever," I said. And despite the fact I maybe should have pursued it further instead of walking away, I turned my back on him and left him there.

CHAPTER THIRTY

I WALKED INTO A heated conversation between Crew and Olivia as the pair faced off in the foyer. Obviously her press conference had ended and for some reason she and her sheriff were at odds again. I was almost at the point I didn't care why anymore, except the amused expression on my dad's face made me pause and want to know what the joke might be.

I could use a laugh right about then.

It was clear enough from the first sentence she uttered I could actually make out what the fuss was about.

"How dare you ask me such questions, Sheriff Turner." She literally huffed like a bull, shoulders twitching inside her precise suit coat. "Or accuse me in any way of murdering our very special guest. I can have you fired for such insolence." Her eyes flickered to me, only then noticing I'd joined them, something I didn't like at all flashing there before she spoke again, hurried and passionate. "Fee was in the carriage with him, not me. Why aren't you asking her questions?"

Did Olivia just try to throw me under the bus? I should have been furious, but all I could do was snort in shock and shake my head while Crew scowled at me then her.

"Fiona had no reason to kill Skip," he said. "And you didn't answer me, Mayor Walker." Crew's temper flared at last. I didn't often see him angry with anyone aside from me, so it was interesting to watch with an outsider's perspective. Yup, there was the left eye twitch and, right on cue, the forehead vein. So this was no show for her benefit. "Why didn't you disclose the termination of contract to your own police department?"

"Because I wasn't taking no for an answer," she snarled. "All right? I was still in negotiations with Evelyn, trying to get Skip to change his mind. And the fact he came with Willow for the shoot made me think he had done just that."

"Except," I said, "it turned out he only came to humiliate us and make a mess of the whole campaign."

Olivia flinched. "The council agreed to give me latitude," she said.

"So the council knew." Crew's anger was gone. Face cold and impassive suddenly. Entire body tense. "But I didn't warrant a need to know."

She paused a long moment, the heat of anger between them now a chill that reached me from across the foyer.

"I'm doing the job you hired me to do," Crew said, shutting down almost completely, a solid mask settling over his features, a deeply cold and professional tone echoing from his voice. "And I am more than willing to speak directly to the town council about my present position if it comes into question. But from now on I will demand the kind of respect for what I'm trying to do for this town to be the norm, Mayor Walker, and not the exception."

Even Dad looked floored and then troubled as Crew spun and walked away from her and stalked from the foyer and into the kitchen.

"Olivia." I didn't realize Mom had joined us until I heard that deeply disappointed tone in the single word she spoke.

Our mayor didn't respond aside from flinching slightly.

"I would hope," Dad said, walking past her toward the kitchen himself, "the damage you've just done to your relationship with our county's sheriff isn't permanent, Olivia. Because I'll tell you one thing." He paused and looked back over his shoulder, looming over me as he did. "He's the best cop I've ever had the luck to work with and you're a fool to cut him out when you should be asking for his help."

Dad left then, Olivia glaring, but between her, Mom and me, the feeling of desperate regret was palpable.

"I had it handled," Olivia said like that fixed everything.

"You certainly did," Mom said. "Everyone's completely impressed, Olivia." She left me there, not hurrying but returning to the kitchen herself. I should have gone with her, but the train wreck unfolding in front of me felt like something someone needed to watch.

"They don't understand," Olivia said. "The pressure I'm under."

I shrugged. "Maybe not. But that doesn't give you permission to treat the people who are trying to help you like crap, Olivia. You're lucky if the council doesn't agree with Crew on this. Especially if anyone else of influence decides to speak up about what happened." Did she realize the position she'd put our town in? "You set us up to look like idiots. I've been on your side for the most part, happy to see Reading on the map. But there comes a time when the pursuit of more leads you down a dark road. And I think you're on it."

My turn to exit stage left. I had no idea if she actually heard me but it wasn't my job to make her understand. Or to educate her, even. She had to learn for herself there were lines you didn't cross. And keeping secrets like this from those who needed to know—to the detriment of everything you yourself had built—was beyond misguided.

Might be time for an election.

I found Mom, Dad, Crew and Daisy drinking coffee in my kitchen, Petunia at my father's feet, eagerly gulping down the bits of cinnamon cake he fed her. He glanced up, a guilty look on his face, and stopped immediately but the lip smacking and bulging eyes of my pug told me he'd been at it long enough she wasn't going to take no for an answer.

Her farts at least would be legendary.

Mom's face fell as she topped up the sheriff's coffee. "Crew—"

"Do me a favor, Flemings," he said before nodding to my best friend, "and Daisy. Let's talk about the case and not whether I'm going to quit my job and walk out on Olivia Walker."

"Can we at least agree she's not a suspect?" Dad sounded like that amused him greatly. "Though I wouldn't tell her that just yet."

"And I think Fee can be off the list," Mom said in a prim tone, my favorite mug full and ready. I took it from her, saluted and sipped. "Ditto for myself, I think. And Daisy? Dear, did you kill the football star monster man?"

She snorted, lips twisting. "Can't say after hearing what I heard about him I wouldn't have helped," she said, "but no. I'm clean."

"Excellent." Mom beamed at us so brightly even Crew chuckled at her enthusiasm. "Now, who's left?"

"I know you disagree, Fee," the sheriff said, "but I like Willow for this. And not just because she's the obvious choice."

"Actually," I said, feeling the sorrow of my admission as I spoke, "I'm kind of with you. She's at the top of the pile."

"Any fingerprints on the bottle or syringe Fee found?" Dad must have forgotten to feel guilty because he was back to feeding Petunia with an absent look on his face. I smacked his arm and he stopped, quick grin belying the earlier regret.

He didn't have to deal with her epic farts in the middle of the night.

"Nothing," Crew said. "Wiped clean."

"Can we agree Evelyn is too smart to leave evidence in the bathroom only she has access to?" I met four pairs of eyes.

"Though," Daisy said after a long silence, hesitant but braver than I'd ever seen her, "wouldn't that be very smart? To make it look like she wasn't guilty?"

"A double blind." I grinned at her and she lost her reluctant quietness and smile back. "You're getting good at this."

"I should deputize the lot of you permanently," Crew said. Why did that statement send a zing of yes please down my spine?

"So, everyone knew Skip was on painkillers. Which means everyone knew how to push him over the edge." Mom tapped the rim of her coffee cup with one fingertip.

"But only a few people had access to Quexol," I said.

"Evelyn, Matt. Skip. And possibly Willow." Crew sipped his coffee, so calm I wondered if he was really okay or not.

"Three suspects," Dad said. "And we're no closer to an answer."

CHAPTER THIRTY-ONE

I REALLY WASN'T IN the mood to help Mom make lunch, but there wasn't much else to be done at the moment. Dad and Crew retreated, Daisy staying with us to help out. No, the whole women in the kitchen thing wasn't lost on me, but I didn't have anything to contribute to the investigation that my poor, tired brain could produce so I instead chopped aggressively at vegetables and tried not to think about the murder.

A nice distraction entered the room in the form of Carter Melnick. He'd traded out his dark suit for jeans and a long sleeved blue shirt, the deep V-neck of the collar showing off his muscular chest in a way that made me blush just for looking.

"Is Willow all right?" Mom paused with a tray of cookies in her hands, dessert for after ready to go in the oven. I know she likely didn't mean to sound like she was judging him for being here instead of there, but Carter shrugged and smiled that winning smile at her, his hands sliding into his back pockets while Daisy did her best not to stare.

Jealous of my bestie? No way. Okay, a little. Growl.

"She made me come back and watch over the others," he said. "She has Jill and two state troopers guarding her. Ms. Pink can be quite forceful even when she's not feeling well. I figured obeying her orders might lead to keeping my job."

Mom nodded and turned to slide the tray into the oven. "Smart boy," she said.

"I'm happy to help serve again, Mrs. Fleming." So polite. Mom didn't seem opposed to the idea and Daisy was doing her best not to flirt. I could tell it was on her mind, but when she looked at him looking at me all instincts to explore that idea died in her eyes. She winked at me and left the kitchen, handing him her knife and letting him finish her job while she left us to the task.

And that was why I loved her so very much. *Best* best friend ever in the history of best friends. I'd have to buy her a plaque. Or a bottle of wine. Or her own island.

"Thanks for the help," I said, loving that he tucked in next to me, hip almost touching mine, our knives rocking over the mix of veggies Mom required at the same pace. It felt natural and all together familiar. I rather liked it.

"I used to waiter in another life," he laughed, deep voice vibrating between us. "I kind of miss it." He paused, looked around. "It's really nice you and your parents can work together so well." He sounded wistful and like he wished he had that sort of relationship.

"This isn't our typical arrangement," I said. "My staff ran for the hills when you lot arrived." I actually hoped the Jones sisters were enjoying their self-made vacation. Put their feet up, ate some junk food and watched soap operas or sappy movies until this was over. At least someone in this mess might have a good time.

"But we don't mind lending a hand when Fee needs us." Wow, did she have a point she was making? I'd never seen my mother like this before, all officially sweet but with a warning under every word she spoke.

Well, she'd commented she worried he might be like Ryan. So I guess it was fair enough. Still, she could cut me a bit of slack and let me see where this might go. Not that it had much potential. I felt the wind leave my sails as I accepted he'd be gone shortly anyway, so why did it matter?

"Do you like working for Willow?" Might as well tear the band aid off and let him stab me in the heart and get it over with.

"Very much," he said. "It's been... educational, to say the least."

"How long have you been in her employ?" Ah. Now I understood Mom's tone. That was the moment her snippy undertone made total sense to me. Because it raised a red flag in my own soul I should have flown high long ago.

"Only two weeks," he said and I instantly exhaled my distress that he might be a part of the Skip problem. "The guy before me just vanished." He shrugged. "They were in a bind so they hired me from the agency." Bodyguards used temp agencies? Huh. "I wish I'd known he was so cruel to her before I took the job."

"So you could turn it down?" Mom wasn't even trying to hide her frustration now, the tray of sandwiches she'd assembled shivering as she set it down more firmly than was necessary.

"No," he said in a soft voice. "So I could have protected her. By the time they hired me to watch her, she was on set and he wasn't around much. I didn't find out about the abuse until they got here. Or I'd have done something about it."

He sounded intimately angry, as if he had some experience with men who hit women. I set my knife down and touched his wrist, his fingers unclenching from the fist he'd made around his own. Carter looked up and met my eyes, his fury as genuine as mine.

"Carter." Mom hesitated then sighed. "I'm sorry, dear."

He shook his head, managed to smile and swallow some of his anger. "It's okay, Mrs. Fleming. I'd jump to that conclusion, too. But that man was a menace from what little interaction I had with him. I'm just happy I was able to be there for Ms. Pink in even a small capacity."

"I know you haven't been with them long," I said. "But if you had to guess, Carter..."

He exhaled heavily. "Who do I think killed him?" He seemed to ponder that question carefully, though surely like the rest of us he'd been thinking about it since it happened. "I don't know enough to say," he whispered. "But if I were the cops, I'd be asking who hated him the most." He seemed to snap out of his moment of focus and shrugged. "But if you're looking for me to point the finger at Ms. Pink, I won't do it."

"I wouldn't want you to," I said.

His answering smile made me warm inside. Down Fee. Pursue the hot guy *after* the murder was solved.

My phone dinged, pulling me away from Mr. Delicious who chatted with Mom in a much friendlier tone while I dodged out into the garden to check the text.

Might have what you're looking for. The number came up unlisted. *Football can be a killer.*

Who the hell is this? I scowled at my phone and awareness triggered before the reply came back.

Russell, Red. Meet me in our spot tonight after 8. Come alone and I'll tell you everything.

We'll see. And though I didn't hear back, glaring into the spring sunshine while I waited for the answering text that never came, I knew I'd be out here, behind the fence and meeting Randy Russell tonight. Because I couldn't help myself.

CHAPTER THIRTY-TWO

THE REST OF THE day seemed to pass in a blur, and by the time Crew grudgingly stopped interrogating the remaining guests and returned to his office to talk to Mila Martin again, I was ready for bed even though it was only 7PM. We were running low on food supplies, though at least the collection of agents, coach and bodyguard who remained with us seemed to enjoy Mom's cooking. I didn't hear any complaints, at least. Maybe they weren't willing to speak up when Dad hovered in his looming and protective way.

They preferred instead to gripe about their circumstances, Evelyn and Julian both spending most of their mealtimes on their phones, Matt sitting in dejected silence, Carter off to one corner by himself observing like a good bodyguard. I was tempted to sit with him for my own meals but got the impression he was working despite his more casual attire and let him be.

Down, girl.

I took the opportunity to make the rounds like I usually did, checking in on towels and toilet paper, leaving fresh pillowcases by their doors without checking inside. I could have. It would have been easy enough to sneak in and peek around. But I knew anything I found would set Crew off as inadmissible due to illegal search. The bathroom on the third floor was a communal area, so that had been fair game. But to go poking around in the suspect's bedrooms without cause—especially since I wasn't deputized yet, damn him—was a useless endeavor.

Besides, I was well aware Dad and Crew had already gone through their belongings. Those two wouldn't have left a stone unflipped, so the odds I'd uncover something new were pretty slim.

Tempting, but nope. Look at me, being a good girl. Crew needed to appreciate me more.

Petunia wandered after me as she always did, sitting when I stopped for more than a step, heaving herself to her feet and plodding along when I moved on. Despite my best efforts to reduce her chubby self to a more acceptable weight, Mom, Dad and, I suspected, the Jones sisters were making my job nearly impossible.

I finally returned downstairs to find my guests huddling in separate unhappiness and my parents in the sitting room on the sofa, holding hands and standing watch. I hated to interrupt them, but Petunia happily hopped up on the couch and made herself comfortable. My intrusion was hardly noteworthy after pug butt assault.

"Daisy called. She's picking up supplies." Mom seemed relaxed enough, though I knew both my parents were accustomed enough to tense situations—she a retired high school principal and he an ex-sheriff—that even if a bomb was about to go off it would take the last ten seconds ticking down for either of them to let me see their terror.

"Thanks, Mom." I hesitated. Really should tell Dad about Randy Russell. And decided to find out what the reporter had to say on my own first before I decided if it was worth taking to Crew. "Can you babysit Petunia a bit? I'm going to do some paperwork."

"Of course, sweetie," Mom said.

"We've got this," Dad nodded.

I left them there, retreated downstairs and did as I said I'd do. I could hear movement over my head occasionally, the scraping of a chair in the dining room as one or another of the suspects vacated to the stairs. The house had a heartbeat to it that was difficult to miss and, by the time I sorted through another pile of emails that I had to turn down, the grandfather clock's tolling of the hour of 8PM almost didn't stir me.

My phone buzzed, jerking me alert and I swore softly before checking the message. But it wasn't Randy Russell chewing me out for missing our meeting. The text was from Jill.

Crew told me to check in. Willow's fine and Mila Martin lawyered up. He'll be back in ten minutes or so to relieve your parents. Round the clock watch until Willow is able to answer more questions.

Thanks, Jill. I stood, pocketing my phone, heading upstairs and creeping into the kitchen. Empty. Mom and Dad had to still be in the sitting room and from the quiet in the dining area everyone else went upstairs. Knowing my parents would kick my butt if they knew what I was about to do, I took a deep breath and went outside, the light triggering over the door as my appearance set it off.

At least I wasn't heading to this clandestine meeting in total darkness. That made it a smart choice, right? And I had my phone in case anything went wrong. I paused by the koi pond, Fat Benny slowly circling the edge, and predialed Crew before tucking my phone back in my pocket. Shook my head at the choice of numbers and hurried on toward the fence, telling myself with every step this was a terrible idea and I'd clearly lost my mind.

The light over the carriage house woke at the exact instant I felt a chill up my spine. Wait, was there someone here? Likely Randy, looking for me. But no, when I paused and looked around, the garden was empty. So empty, in fact, the light over the kitchen door flickered and went out.

Second thoughts whispered in my mind. Yes, there was illumination by the carriage house. But once I passed that fence, I was heading into who knew what. Still, it wasn't like Randy Russell was going to murder me or anything, right? He wasn't the killer. Was he?

I had an overactive imagination that really needed to give me a break right about now.

My phone buzzed and this time I knew it had to be the reporter. Taking a deep breath, I plunged toward the fence, jaw tight against my fear and the need to turn and run back to the main house as fast as my legs would carry me like a terrified little girl who couldn't stand the dark.

I had just enough momentum to make it to the fence break before my breath caught and good sense stopped me in my tracks. It would take two seconds to call Dad. He'd come and we'd talk to Randy together. What the hell was I thinking? When Crew found out his eye twitch and forehead vein would be the least of my worries.

Heart pounding, decision made, I half turned toward the yard just as the light over the carriage house died. I froze, heart a terrified rabbit stock still in my chest, as someone rushed toward me, a bulky shadow, so fast I didn't have time to use the deep breath I inhaled to scream.

Light burst behind my eyes, pain exploding in the back of my head, darkness swallowing me immediately thereafter.

CHAPTER THIRTY-THREE

SOMETHING WET TOUCHED MY face, not once but many times, sticky and hot. I tried to bat it away but my hands didn't seem to work through the bursting violence of the pain in my head and how my entire body seemed to be detached from that pain.

Or consumed by it. Hard to make the distinction while my eyes ached with the effort to open them, voices calling my name going in and out, bright lights turning to darkness and back again while that endless wetness went on and on.

"Fee." I managed to blink through the agony at last, the groan that sounded like a zombie rising from her grave tearing a wet hole through the seal in my parched throat. I finally managed to lift my hand and felt Petunia's wet nose press into my fingers, her soft whining reaching me through the buzzing hum of my hurt.

"Call an ambulance, now." That sounded like Crew, or was it Dad? They had similar voices, those sheriffs, all husky and commanding. I faded out, darkness taking me again until whoever was saying my name in my ear got through and I resurfaced.

"Mom." I croaked that at her, something hot and wet landing on my cheek and I realized I'd made her cry. "'Sokay, Mom."

"Where is that ambulance?" Wait, was that Pamela? What was she doing here? She looked down at me, so hard to focus on her worried face, light from overhead flaring in my eyes. "Hang in there, Fee. You're going to be all right."

Why did she sound like she was trying to convince herself as well as me?

This was ridiculous. I had to sit up. This weird devouring pain had to go away, would vanish if I could just sit up. But the instant I tried, my entire head exploded with more fireworks and the black that devoured me was a welcome retreat.

The next time I blinked awake to the sounds and sights of the outside world, I was indoors, in the familiar comfort of the sitting room, though comfort was a relative term. At least this time I didn't feel so out of it, my return to consciousness the sharp edges of reality instead of the wavering wonky trip that had been the backyard.

"Fee." Mom was there, holding my hand, Petunia looking up at me from where someone had laid me out on the couch. "The ambulance is coming, sweetie. Any second now."

"What happened?" I'm not sure those words were audibly coherent, though they seemed okay in my head when I said them.

Pamela was talking in the background, almost whispering but just loud enough to hear. "I found her that way. I didn't see anything."

Dad appeared in my view, sitting on the edge of the sofa and trying a grim smile that didn't reach his eyes. "We were hoping you could tell us that."

"It's here." Crew burst into the room, looking panicked, stricken. And seemed hesitant when Dad lifted me into his arms, as if he wanted to protest my father's gesture. I wanted to tell them both I could walk, thanks, except, yeah. I didn't think I really could so I shut up and tried not to whimper as the pain rolled over me in fresh waves and everything wobbled back into black.

Third waking was the charm, apparently. Soft beeping stirred me from unconsciousness, the harsh scent of industrial cleaners, the sound of voices and someone paging Dr. Hippler to the E.R. The hospital? I groaned as I tried for the last time to sit up and was immediately pushed down again, gently. Didn't take much strength to hold me in place, either. I felt like someone wrung me out and shook me until I was empty.

"Just stay with us a few minutes, sweetie, if you can." Mom's hands touched my cheeks. "You have a concussion and Dr. Aberstock wants you to sleep." Wait, wasn't that wrong? Didn't I have to stay awake? Apparently not. Weird for my brain to argue silently while I struggled to even pay attention to her. "But your Dad and Crew have some questions first." She sounded like she thought they could wait. "Okay?"

I nodded, huge mistake. Almost cried it hurt so much. Breathed through the pain while Mom sat back and a nicely smiling young nurse in dark blue scrubs stabbed my I.V. with a needle and emptied her syringe into the line.

"Try to stay quiet," the nurse said. "I'll be back to check on you." She left, Crew stepping aside when he appeared at the door, letting her slip past him before coming inside, his face twisted in worry.

"She's going to be fine." That was Dad from the other side of my bed. I didn't turn my head to look at him, knowing it would hurt too much. Daisy appeared over Mom's shoulder, waved a little, biting at her lower lip and looking like she wanted to cry.

Crew approached, hat in his hands, dark hair in desperate need of a cut hanging over his blue eyes. "Do you know what happened, Fee?"

I didn't shake my head this time, trying to lick my lips past the pasty dryness. Mom immediately offered me a glass with a bendy white straw and I managed to suck in a bit without choking myself before answering.

"It was my own stupid fault," I said, my voice sounding like I'd been gargling heavy grit sandpaper. "Randy Russell, the paparazzo? He told me he had information for me that might help the case, but he refused to meet me if I didn't come alone."

It was almost a good thing I was hurt, because the four people staring down at me in varying degrees of shock and fury would likely have killed me themselves if I wasn't lying in that hospital bed.

Mom seemed to recover first, her face settling as she shot a glare at the two sheriffs before returning her attention to me. "We'll talk about your brilliant life choices later," she said, triggering my funny bone and making me giggle before I groaned at the agony of it.

"Please don't make me laugh," I whispered. "I'm sorry. I know it was dumb."

"Did he attack you?" Crew almost bounced on his toes, Dad suddenly standing next to him, the pair of them looking like a hit squad waiting for their Don to tell them who to ice.

"I don't know," I said. "Whoever hit me was on our side of the fence. They knew about the motion lights."

"They were both broken," Dad said, as grim as I'd ever heard him. "If it wasn't for Pamela, we might not have found you until we went to bed and that could have been hours."

"And Petunia," Mom said. "I was letting her out to do her business when Pamela called for us. That pug ran right to you." My mother sniffed, took a moment to collect herself as emotion washed over her face. I felt like a total heel for scaring her like this. But she managed to go on. "Thank goodness you're all right."

"I have to go back to Petunia's," Crew said, looking frustrated, vibrating with it. "Willow's been released and I have more questions for her."

"Find Randy," I said. "I have no idea if his information is important. But whoever hit me had to be following me."

"Or lured you out there," Dad said. "Leave it to us, kid."

Like I had a choice. If I wasn't in so much pain I would have been irritated to watch the two men go without me. Instead, I did my best to close my eyes and sleep as the pain finally retreated and the mercy of whatever the nurse gave me carried me back into oblivion.

CHAPTER THIRTY-FOUR

IT WAS A FITFUL night of being woken often, though when I finally opened my eyes for real and not in a mumbling state of protest, it wasn't to the nice nurse in the blue scrubs with more medication, but to my dad sitting at my side, holding my hand.

I winced into the early morning light coming through the edges of the blinds, but the longer I looked at him, the more the pain of that illumination faded.

Dad's smile reminded me of the times I'd gotten hurt as a little girl, all sweet and kind of goofy around the edges, like he didn't quite know how to comfort me.

"Thanks for being here," I whispered, voice cracking. "I know Crew probably needs you. And you didn't get any sleep, did you?"

Dad patted my hand, blinking a few times a bit too fast while his throat worked before he spoke. "Everything's under control, Fee. You just rest."

"I'd rather go home." I actually felt a lot better for sleeping, though I'd had a mild concussion once in high school when I tried out for the girl's rugby team and realized quickly I was far too competitive for my own good. Hadn't they forced me to stay awake that time? I was grateful that had been kyboshed. Sleeping was much preferable to sitting up in woozy, nauseated silence. That time it had taken a giant tackle of an opposing team member and an impact with the goal post and my noggin to make my decision for me that maybe rugby wasn't my game. I'd been out of commission for a week, lots of popsicles and Mom love and another two months or so of forgetting common word meanings and occasional fainting spells.

This felt way worse.

"Crew's about to release Willow's people," Dad said, frustration creeping into his voice. Not that anyone but a Fleming would recognize it, but it was there. "He's decided she's his prime suspect after all and is going to hand her over to the state troopers to wrap things up."

"Let me guess," I said. "Olivia."

"She's under a lot of pressure," Dad said. "While good press is good for business and murder doesn't seem to turn people away, I think the council has had enough of the circus hanging around outside Petunia's and taking over our town." He sighed, hands tightening on mine a moment before he managed a smile again. "Betty and Mary are back at the B&B, so you don't have to worry. And Daisy is with them. She's got things handled. So you can just rest for now. And get better."

"This isn't my first kick at the bucket, Dad," I said.

"I know." He stilled a bit, swallowed. "They did a CT scan while you were unconscious. No swelling on your brain." Now he was breaking down, cracking around the edges like Mom had last night. It took him longer to make it through the wave of emotion that gripped him so tightly while I held still and let him process. "So you'll likely be getting your wish if Dr. Aberstock clears you to go home."

Amazing he could just carry on with the last of the conversation after that massive battle with his fear.

"Dad." I didn't know what to say. Flemings weren't big on displays of emotion.

"Your mother and I are going to help with Petunia's," he said, nodding like that was going to start an argument. "Feels good to be there anyway, like I'm close to Mom again." He looked like that was painful too and I wondered if he'd ever really processed his mother's death. Having me at Petunia's must have raised a lot of feelings he, as big and strong John Fleming, wasn't prepared to handle with emotion. "Lloyd said the more rest you get the faster you'll heal."

I couldn't help the tears that trickled from my eyes, the swelling of my own terror, woken now that I was safe and out of immediate danger and with my father sitting next to me like I'd broken his heart and he was only now trying to glue the pieces back together without showing me how shattered he'd been.

"I'm sorry." An ugly sob escaped, making me gasp from the pain.

Dad's face crumpled. I'd done him in the rest of the way, I guess. Together, his head bent over my hand, we cried as one, tied tightly by the entwined fingers of our grasping hands.

"Don't you ever," he whispered in a hoarse voice as we both recovered, "scare me like that again. Fee. I thought it was bad when you told me about the attack on Valentine's Day." Right. Seemed like having my life put in danger was a bit of a habit since I got home, though this time there was no quick recovery with coffee and a warm fire after a near death experience in a snowstorm. "But by the time you told me you were more angry than afraid." If only he'd known how frightened I was that night, but I guess I hid it as well as he taught me to. "Seeing you lying there in the garden." Dad choked again, looked away. "I don't know what I'd do if something happened to you."

More tears, but these were good ones, at least as far as I was concerned. I'd left Reading eleven years ago now, an angry young woman with a chip on my shoulder and some harsh words for both of my parents. Words I knew they didn't deserve, that they'd done their best over the years to nurture and protect me and I'd paid them back with disdain and left them behind, just like I'd left Daisy behind.

Coming home had healed some of the breach and we'd never actually talked about how I'd left. Because Flemings. It was as if my parents auto forgave everything I'd said, bless them, and we started where we'd left off before my stomping exit from Reading with my stuff in my beat up car and college and my future more important than the people who raised me.

This felt like I was finally healing the gap between my father and me, the giant chasm I'd created when I left to start a life that gave me nothing but frustration and hurt. Lying there, loving my father, I would have given anything to rewind the years, to shake the girl I'd been for being so selfish and ridiculous, for blaming him for keeping me from my dream when I was the coward. I could have gone to the academy, but I let my own fears hold me back.

My fault.

I didn't get to say all that to Dad, because the door whispered wider, a familiar face smiling tentatively at me while Pamela wavered at the entry as if wondering if she was welcome. Dad and I both wiped at our wet faces, my father rising quickly, pausing to kiss my forehead for a moment before leaving the room in long, ground eating strides and leaving me wishing he'd just come back again and never, ever leave me alone.

CHAPTER THIRTY-FIVE

TURNED OUT DAD AND I weren't the only weepy ones. Pamela hurried to me when Dad left and hugged me, tears on her face. I was surprised the tough as nails newspaper reporter showed such emotion then remembered she'd been the one who found me.

"Thanks for the rescue," I whispered. She gave me some water, thankfully without me having to ask, the bendy straw delivering tepid liquid better than any coffee or wine I'd ever tasted.

"I wish I'd gotten there sooner." She sat next to me, glass in her lap, face strained and tired. "I was snooping, heading to see you, if you had anything new." Pamela dashed at the tears on her cheeks, one hand supporting the frosted plastic glass, liquid sloshing over the side and into her lap. She didn't seem to notice. "I saw that Randy Russell, the paparazzo." Her nose wrinkled. "He rushed past me when I was on my way to the edge of the fence. Fee, I have no idea if he attacked you, but he looked like the devil was chasing him." Her hand clenched into a fist around the glass, making the plastic creak. "If I had known I would have tackled him and not let him go, the weasel. But he was long gone by the time I found you and all I could think of was you were dead and I started screaming for help." She sobbed softly before shaking herself and swallowing hard. "I'm so glad you're all right."

Wow. Way to make me emotional all over again. "My hero." I managed a smile and she laughed through her tears.

"Silly," she said. "I hear you're the heroic one. Going out there alone to get information."

"Um, I think everyone else would clarify that choice as stupid ass," I said.

She patted my hand, offered me the straw almost absently. "You'd make a good reporter. You ever decide to give it a go, you let me know. I like your instincts."

Hmmm. Something to consider. Though with the death of Skip Anderson I was confident the rooms at Petunia's would be packed for the next two years in a row.

Someone knocked, gaining our attention. I really needed to remember not to turn my head so fast, gasping a little as the world wobbled slightly. Crew waited at the door, hesitating as Pamela had hesitated with Dad, and the newswoman did as my father had, leaping to her feet, setting aside the glass before waving and hurrying out.

The sheriff let her go with a nod, drifting closer but not sitting down just yet. Why did he look so uncomfortable, his hands shifting around and around the brim of his hat, his eyes downcast, his shoulders slumped?

"I'm just checking in before I head back to town," he said. "Your dad told you about Willow?"

"I don't think she did it," I said. "I think whoever hit me either killed Skip or knows who did and is protecting the murderer."

Crew sighed, sank at last into the chair beside me. "I agree," he said. "But as soon as I get back I have to hand her over to the troopers, Fee. Unless I have evidence otherwise, she'll have to face more questions and possibly charges if they don't come up with a reason to look elsewhere." He perked a bit. "Good news, though. Lloyd gave the go ahead to release you. Said you'll heal better at home." That *was* good news. "I don't want you to worry. The troopers might have Willow, but I'm not going to let Randy Russell get away with this."

"You think it was him?" Why would he lure me out there when he had the chance to hurt me twice already? And yet, he hadn't exactly been forthcoming with the information he claimed to have, and had made me come to see him alone in the dark. So maybe he was behind my attack.

But what possible reason would the paparazzo with a restraining order against him from a man who hated his guts and who he supposedly hated have to hurt me and protect who killed Skip?

"Do you think he did it?" I cleared my throat and realized I needed to clarify. "Do you think he's the murderer?"

Crew hesitated. "I know there was no love lost between them. But motive, Fee. I just don't see it." He rubbed between his eyes with two fingers, weariness showing. When he met my gaze again, he seemed to snap out of his sharing mode and into protectiveness again. "Like I said, I don't want you to worry. You need to focus on getting better."

I let him go without protesting because even if I wanted to fight him on being part of the case or not, it appeared that option had been taken from me twofold. Not only was I in enough pain I really shouldn't be thinking about who murdered Skip but with the loss of the investigation to the state troopers, there was nothing left to figure out.

The rest was up to them, apparently.

Mom and Daisy took Crew's place a few minutes later. I was glad to see them, if only to silence the terrible voice in my head that whispered to me what a mess I'd made of things. And that promised me it would find a night or two along the way to add to my list of growing nightmares that jerked me awake and made me hug my pug tight while I fought the pounding of my terrified heart.

Something fabulous to look forward to.

Dr. Aberstock's quick visit cleared me with his characteristic grin and an offer of a green lollipop that made me smile. How had he remembered my favorite after all these years? I sucked the sugar, the only thing I'd had to eat for almost twelve hours, and took my time getting dressed, letting Mom and Daisy do most of the work. Nor did I fight the wheelchair the orderly used to push me to the front door, or argue against the help they gave me into the back seat of Mom's car.

Petunia pounced on me the second I was inside, rattling my brain a bit too much for comfort, but I snuggled her anyway, breathing through the nausea that movement caused in the scent of her fur.

I honestly don't remember the drive home or how I got inside. I vaguely recall Betty hugging me, then Mary, the two acting about as uncharacteristically emotional as my dad had, though there was precedent as the sisters had broken down when they admitted they worried I was going to fire them way back in July.

Mom and Daisy were amazing, got me into pajamas, then into bed, a pair of pills pressed into my hand. I had no idea if they were Vicodin, had no reason to believe they were, but as I swallowed them with a sip of water and sank back into my pillows, the journey home almost too much for me to stay awake a second longer, I thought about Willow and Skip and my mind whispered I was forgetting something, wasn't I? Something important.

It would have to wait for tomorrow. The second Petunia settled next to me, her soft snoring a lulling sound in the dark while Mom drew the curtains to cut off the light, I drifted into the peace offered by the painkillers and forgot I forgot until I opened my eyes into the next day.

And remembered.

CHAPTER THIRTY-SIX

I GUESS I SHOULDN'T have been surprised to find Daisy on my sofa again, or her softly caring way of hovering around me as I made coffee—probably a bad idea to pour caffeine on a concussion, but whatever—and tried to go about my morning routine like nothing happened.

Made worse when Mom appeared, tsking at my cup of java, offering up two pills I swallowed reluctantly but knew if I was going to manage to function today past the pain I had to have them. And finally exhaled in irritation at the pair of them as they stared at me in anxious silence as if any second now I'd keel over and require assistance.

"Thank you," I said, standing on shaking knees and gently but firmly guiding them both to the stairs. "But unless you plan to have a shower with me—no thanks!—you two can do me a huge solid and go upstairs and make sure this place isn't falling apart."

That worked, giving them something to do. But the mournful expression on Daisy's face as she left, Petunia going with her, and Mom's worried glances back over her shoulder were pretty clear indications I was in for a rough ride with them. This level of care from my friends and family was going to drive me around the bend.

I took my time in the shower, going slow, wincing when I washed my hair and tried not to touch the spot where the blow from the garden shovel Crew informed me the attacker used left a huge lump. Fortunately, my red mane was thick enough the handle didn't split my scalp so I didn't need stitches. But that didn't seem to make much difference when it came to the ache and I wondered maybe if whoever hit me had opened my skull the pain would have had a place to go...?

Silly pondering, but a distraction from what I really needed to think about. The fact I'd somehow managed to shunt aside the story Matt and Evelyn told me about the young football up and comer and his untimely suicide.

Considering there were no other leads to pursue, it nagged at me, poking me here and there inside my sore and weary noggin while I contemplated shaving my legs before snorting at the very idea of bending over. I'd just have to stay hairy a few days.

By the time I toweled off, dizzy and a bit sick but glad to be clean, dressed and bundled my still damp and unbrushed hair into a disastrous bun at the base of my neck, I was ready to go back to bed. And had to sit down for a minute, more coffee to the rescue, while I tried one last time to sort through what had been plaguing me since I woke up.

The concussion and painkillers made it so hard to focus I actually had a flash of sympathy for Skip. Just a brief blip, mind you, a hiccup of solidarity in the face of this hideous feeling of detachment and wobbliness tied to a dull ache that I knew was way worse but I just didn't process it right now thanks to the drugs. I could only imagine what the football star had felt after a lifetime of injuries and an overabundance of access to pain meds. How it could alter his personality, augment his natural violent tendencies. I certainly didn't feel myself and to have this become the norm rather than the exception?

My entire body shuddered in response to the thought, making me wince and then flinch. I just wanted to feel human again and it had barely been a day.

I finally sighed into the empty mug in my hand and shrugged off the nagging thoughts about the dead young football star. Research into his situation was in order, but maybe I'd just pass it on to Crew. The idea of actually focusing on anything felt like about the biggest stretch ever and I just didn't have it in me.

The stairs were impossibly long, and I was panting after three breaks by the time I reached the foyer. No way was I letting Mom or Dad or Daisy see me like this, let alone the Jones sisters. Though why I was being so stubborn about getting up I had no idea. Sense of responsibility, I guess, the familiarity of this place I now called home. I'd rest later, sleep and hopefully escape the ache and the wavering discomfort that was my world. But, for now, I needed to move.

I was surprised to find the kitchen empty, no sign of Mom or Betty. I moved with shuffling feet inside my slip on sneakers, feeling about as ancient as the two ladies who worked for me, maybe more, hating the slump of my shoulders and the moan worthy turtle speed that dragged at me while I forced one foot in front of the other.

Okay, maybe I really did need to go back to bed.

Someone knocked at the kitchen door, making me squeal and jump. I had to get a handle on that reaction to surprise, but after the few days I'd had I hoped no one would blame me for it. And didn't really give a crap if they did.

When I turned, I was shocked to find Mila Martin peeking in the screen, her glasses flashing with the sunbeam that reached past her shoulder, her face pinched and shoulders as hunched as mine.

"I'm sorry to disturb you, Fee," she said in her small voice, easing her body the rest of the way inside. "Are you okay? I heard about the attack." Her fingers pushed at the bridge of her glasses before clutching together in a little puzzle in front of her as she clasped her hands together.

"I'll be all right," I said. Hesitated. "When did Crew let you out?"

She seemed to understand the implication of my question, maybe heard the edge of fear in my voice.

This wasn't like me, to suspect others of horrible things. Okay, well, perhaps I did. But I wasn't afraid all the time. Was I?

"Late last night," she said. "After."

I nodded, wished I hadn't moved my head, sank into the stool by the counter and sighed. "I'm glad he let you out." Best I could do. "I know you didn't kill Skip."

"And Willow didn't either." She lunged toward me suddenly, her entire being shifting from retreating little mouse to pouncing cat and back again while I caught at the edge of the counter and tried not to meep once more. "I know it. I just need to prove it to those Neanderthals who are trying to take her into custody."

"Wait, trying?" Crew said the troopers were there to take her last night. "She's not gone yet?"

"They're bullying her, but Julian has her barricaded in the station. He's doing his lawyer thing, has a judge on the phone. It's a big mess." She sighed soft and low, like the tragedy that unfolded was the worst thing that ever happened to anyone. "Poor Willow."

"I'm sure they'll get it sorted out." I, on the other hand, just wanted to lower my forehead to my forearms and close my eyes for a second. But Mila didn't move, standing there, staring at me with something that looked like expectation so I guess I had to ask her what she wanted, right?

"I need into Willow's room." I should have expected that and almost laughed, except it would hurt too much. But Mila rushed on, closing the gap between us, her hands on my hands and her stringy brown hair brushing her cheeks as she leaned in when she went on. "Not for trophies, Fee. To find proof she's innocent." She blinked at me through those thick glasses. "I know she's innocent."

Whatever. I shrugged, waved off her grip and tried to care. "Fine." I should have said no, I think, I just couldn't muster it.

She beamed at me, clapped her hands. And grasped my fingers tight in hers, jerking me to my feet. "Come on!"

I don't think she realized how close I was to throwing up on her comfortable looking shoes, or that by the time she had me at the bottom of the stairs that darkness was trying to close in around the edges again. Somehow I made it to the second floor, though like the day before I doubt I'll ever remember the journey. I instead found myself sinking gratefully into the mattress of the four poster queen in the Green Suite, collapsing sideways while Mila puttered around Willow's things.

This was a terrible idea. Where was Mom? Daisy? The Jones sisters? Who let this woman in, anyway? Oh, right. I did. I needed more drugs, apparently.

Mila's face appeared in my view for a moment as she squealed so loudly I sat up, startled, a moment of clarity turning into a tumble to the floor as she dove for the head of the bed and hugged Willow's pillow.

So much for no trophies. My view of her skewed sideways as my torso toppled to the side, my body collapsing all the way to the hardwood floor. I ended up on my back somehow, probably sliding over the slick surface of the newly polished wood and I stared up at the ceiling with its medallion and tasteful chandelier like I'd never seen it before.

At least, not from this perspective. But it was so bright, the sun beaming in on my face, and I turned my head away with a soft groan of protest, into the shadow under the bed. Ah. So much better.

And opened my eyes.

The pointed end of a syringe, uncapped and discarded out of normal view, seemed to give me the finger, a single drop of moisture beaded at the end.

CHAPTER THIRTY-SEVEN

CREW'S ANGER REGISTERED, BUT barely. I just grunted in response to the question he asked, not quite capable at the moment of understanding what it was he wanted from me. He really needed to do something about that vein in his forehead. It was getting bigger over time and might lead to serious medical issues if he wasn't careful.

And hey, why was he mad at me, anyway? Didn't I turn up a piece of evidence for him in my sadly beat up state? Something he and Dad both missed? So there, Sheriff Jerkman Turner. Go suck on that sad popsicle.

"Crew." Dad's intervention startled me, about as much as the realization I was sitting in the front room again. Wait, how did I get here? Oh, right. Mom showed up about a second after I found the syringe and called everyone to come. Or was that screamed? I seemed to recall screaming about me and the floor? Because I had been on the floor. But that was how I found the syringe.

My hands grasped at my head, the ache making it almost impossible to think about anything clearly.

"Here, sweetie." Mom grasped my wrist, forced more pills into my hands, a glass of water. I laid my head back on the sofa a moment, closing my eyes, willing the drugs to work. I don't recall much for the next little bit, but I do remember the moment the pain seemed to recede and I came back to myself. I opened my eyes and wished I hadn't before forcing my body upright.

"Were there fingerprints on the syringe?" I must have interrupted a conversation because the heated whispering going on around me stopped and everyone stared. I blinked at them slowly, the pain waving goodbye, see you later, as it retreated in the wake of the pills. Which just made me wonky, but I'd take it. "Fingerprints." I licked my lips. "People. The syringe from Willow's room."

Dad cleared his throat. "No," he said. "Nothing."

I accepted the water glass from Mom, cleared my mouth with a sip. "So another plant, more than likely."

"Possibly," Crew said. He was pacing and it was making things worse for me when I tried to look at him so I didn't bother, staring instead at the shimmering surface of the liquid in my glass, wondering why I never noticed before how pretty water was in sunlight, the way it refracted into rainbows and bits of sparkles.

Yup. I was officially stoned.

"But." That was Daisy who settled next to me, hand on my leg in an offer of comfort. I lifted my gaze to the pug sitting on my feet, her bulging eyes making me giggle. "It might be enough to shatter this game Julian's playing with the troopers and get Willow arrested."

"Wait," I said. "You didn't hand it over yet?" At least, that's what I meant to say. I think it mostly came out, but not really coherent. But Crew seemed to understand the garbled words enough he shook his head.

"I don't care what Olivia says," he growled. "This is my case."

Ah. Hurt boy pride. Got it.

Something dinged. And dinged again. I knew that sound, nodded as I realized what it was and then wondered why I was nodding to myself over the fact my phone was making noises. I tried to reach for it in my back pocket, feeling the vibration of the device against my skin like something totally alien and utterly shocking. Mom grabbed the glass out of my hand and only then did I realize I'd just let it go. I smiled at her, at least I think I did, fumbling my phone into my lap where I stared down at it and the number on the screen.

"Randy," I said at last.

Dad lunged for my phone, Crew, too, but Mom beat them too it. I peeked around her capable hands as she checked the text, the words bleeding together as she read them.

"*Sorry you were hurt. Had to book.*" She frowned at little at the terminology. "Oh, he means he had to run away."

"You don't have to translate, Lucy," Crew said between gritted teeth. He held one hand out for it but she ignored him and went on.

"Got there after you went down, help was coming. Still have info but don't want to text. You earned it." Mom grunted like she was offended. "I guess so."

Only then did she give Crew my phone. I wasn't sure that was something I was okay with but I really couldn't decide either way.

"Come here. No more cloak and dagger." Crew read as he typed then hit send, the zinging sound of the text departing making my ears ring.

Only a moment passed before it dinged again and he read, *"Tonight."*

No one seemed particularly happy about the delay, but it wasn't like they had much choice. And since I was starting to smell colors—did you know the green of my mother's eyes has the distinct scent of fresh mowed grass?—it was probably just as well.

Sleep was about as welcome as anything I'd ever been offered.

When I woke, it was getting dark outside, the full day lost to rest and recovery. I actually felt better, more alert, but didn't turn down the meds Mom offered. Except, instead of two, I pocketed one and downed the other, hoping for a balance between being doped out of my mind and at a bearable level of pain.

It was still slow going, mind you, but the wonkiness was less and the dizziness had subsided to the point a bit of dry toast and a few mouthfuls of Mom's tomato soup gave me a bit of energy and a warm place in my stomach. And though I knew the others were going to try to bully me into going back to bed, I was firmly seated at the counter when Randy's next text came through.

Back door, I messaged. *We're waiting.*

He had to know I wouldn't be alone, but looked a bit nervous as he slipped through the kitchen door, almost sniffing the air, reminding me of an anxious rabbit checking out the scene before relaxing enough to eat the flowers in my garden. His compact body and dark brown clothing wasn't helping the mental image and I had to fight a wave of hysterical giggles that tried to take me over.

Because giggling was totally appropriate at a time like this.

CHAPTER THIRTY-EIGHT

"**M**R. RUSSELL," CREW SAID, arms crossed over his chest, expression dark and flat. "How kind of you to finally join us."

He tried a grin but it died, his familiar cockiness gone. "I'm sorry about running like that." He directed his apology to me. "I couldn't do anything and I heard someone coming so I knew you'd be okay." Randy swallowed, clearly uncomfortable facing the four people in the kitchen who glared at him with accusing eyes.

I waved off the protective flare of anger that made the kitchen feel like doomsday for the paparazzo photographer and sighed. "Just tell us what you have," I said.

Randy's eyes flickered to the counter beside me, the pile of cookies Mom just made. And this time his grin was real. "I'm starving."

His arrogance knew no bounds, apparently. Mom gestured for him to come closer, seated him with a glass of milk and a pile of chocolate chip melty goodness which Randy stuffed into his now cheerful face before he started talking through crumbs and gulps of moo.

"I think I've been in the game too long," he said. "I should have just told you what I knew. But at first I was looking for reciprocity, some tit-for-tat. Knew the second I met you, Red, that'd never happen. I'd chased the lead I had myself long enough I knew I'd never get anything else out of it. Still, this job makes you squirrely about trusting anyone."

Because he was a snake and a miserable excuse for a human being who uncovered the darkest moments of people's lives and displayed them for the world to see.

Sympathy, thy name is Fiona Fleming.

"Then, when you got hurt. Well, by then I was scared." He stared down at the cookie in his hand like he didn't know what it was before shaking off his excuses and stuffing it in his mouth, chewing once before swallowing and going on. "Thing is, I've been researching Skip for years. Ever since the rat's ass decided he was better at this game than me." Randy laughed, barking a few bits of cookie as he continued to eat. "I've turned up a lot of dirt on that bastard, a lot. Like a book's worth. But the thing that got me stirred up, my paparazzo senses tingling, was the kid who killed himself last year."

Exactly what I'd been thinking about but without success. "Jason Hagan," I said while Crew grunted like I'd kicked him.

Whoops. I failed to mention it, didn't I? But it never seemed relevant before. Annoyingly upsetting, but not tied to the murder since Jason had killed himself. So why was Randy bringing it up?

I explained quickly what Evelyn and Matt told me while Randy nodded endlessly with great enthusiasm, finally slowing his cookie intake after about a dozen to gulp more milk and interrupt.

"Yes to all of this," he said. "Hagan's a big potential star, gets a starting lineup call, Skip hits him intentionally, gets the kid hooked and the rest is history." Randy seemed at first pleased, then pissed off as he realized what he'd said. "The family was devastated. Jason was the first person in their whole clan to make something of himself. Just a freaking tragedy."

"They settled," I said. "Took money to go away." Not that I was accusing them of anything. If Randy was right, they probably saw the money as the only satisfaction they'd ever get.

"They did," he said, sounding sad now. "I tried to convince them otherwise, but the team lawyers got to them and that was it. Game over." Randy sagged in the stool before shaking it off like that same rabbit he resembled until his grin turned him into a fox on the hunt. "Thing is, the mother then dies three months after of a heart attack. But I say a broken heart." He tensed as he went on, like he was preparing for battle. "Dad's an alcoholic, drinking through the measly $50,000 they settled for and big brother's been a drug addict since he was a teenager, disappeared shortly after Mom died and dies, too, in a squatter fire after stealing half the remaining cash and running with it."

I stared at Randy, heart breaking, trying to fathom the level of destruction Skip's selfish and jealous act had triggered. An avalanche of agony and a family laid waste by a man who didn't need to be a monster.

Crew cleared his throat while Mom wiped at her eyes with a murmur of something I didn't catch, turning her back on us with her head bowed. Daisy just swayed, mouth opening and closing, like she searched for something to say in a moment when there was nothing. Nothing.

Dad just scowled at the floor as the sheriff spoke.

"I'll look into it myself," he said. "Do you think the older brother or the father could somehow have found their way here or managed to get some of the Quexol in their possession?"

Randy shrugged, seeming defeated now that he'd finished his tirade. "I don't know," he said. "I've been keeping my eyes open, but from what I know the dad, Abner Hagan, is still in New Jersey. And like I said, the brother is gone. They found a burned out abandoned warehouse squatters frequented with three bodies in it and some of his stuff was there. So he's a dead end, if you pardon the pun."

"But this isn't the first time Skip's done something of the sort, is it?" I met Crew's eyes. "Maybe Randy can give you a list? If there are more victims of his jealousy, maybe one of them decided to act on it when they heard about Jason and his family?"

Long shot. I could see it on Crew's face. And I honestly had to admit it really did look like Willow might be the murderer. But no stone unturned and all that, right?

"I have to turn the evidence into the troopers," he said then, softly, all the fight going out of him. I knew then it didn't matter what Randy said. That the sheriff agreed and whoever hit me was probably trying to protect Willow. So maybe Julian or even Stella. We might never know. And I honestly didn't care at this point. I just wanted it to be over.

Not like me, but there it was.

Randy left, going with Crew to the office, Mom and Dad retiring to their suite in the carriage house. The Jones sisters were already gone and I shooed Daisy off home for the night, promising her I was going right to bed. Now that my special guests were gone, the street outside seemed quiet, peaceful even. Dad's guess the media would want to talk to me thanks to my proximity with Skip's dead body turned out to be less enticing than his wife at the police station, I guess.

I found myself pacing the house, Petunia at my feet, well into the evening, nerves keeping me moving.

Every time I settled down to watch a movie or surf the net or even try to read, my mind spun into fear and anxiety and the pain of focusing on anything just augmented my unsettled feeling.

By the time someone knocked on the front door, I was so wound up I almost didn't answer it, but forced myself to breathe, standing in my foyer with my heart in my throat and my unhappy pug at my feet, pulling every scrap of who I was back together again.

Fiona Fleming wasn't afraid of something as simple as answering her own front door. And the day she let fear stop her from anything was the day she curled up in her dark bedroom and gave up forever.

So there.

With my shoulders squared, I turned the knob at the second soft knock and, plastering a welcoming smile on my trembling lips, I pulled it open. And almost burst into tears at the sight of Carter Melnick standing on my porch with a bouquet of flowers and a worried expression on his handsome face.

CHAPTER THIRTY-NINE

WE ENDED UP ON the couch in the sitting room, his flowers in a vase of water, his arm around my shoulders with the gentlest of pressure, cheek against my hair as I let myself lean into him and did my best not to cry all over his soft cotton shirt. His free hand held one of mine in his lap, the one around me softly stroking my upper arm as he just held me and let me shiver while he supported me without saying a word.

When I finally leaned away I could smile for real, much calmer and more myself than I had been since the attack. Carter touched the point of my chin with one finger before smiling back.

"I'm so sorry, Fee," he said. "This should never have happened to you." Again he touched me, this time over the round of my cheekbone, pushing a bit of hair away, such tenderness in his touch, in his beautiful eyes. I sighed and let my head rest back on his arm, though I winced when I made contact and immediately flinched away. His anxiety flared. "You should be lying down." He tried to rise but I patted his thigh and reassured him with a little lip twist of wry amusement.

"You sound like my mother," I said. "But I'm okay. My head won't stop spinning. I just need to settle a bit then I'll try again."

He relaxed against me, the subtle scent of him not so much warming me up as mellowing me out. Too bad he'd be going back to L.A. soon. I was pretty sure I could get used to this.

"I saw you in the hospital," he said. "After they brought you in. I stopped in to see you but you were out of it." Petunia groaned softly, staring up at both of us but making no effort to leap into his lap. Nice of her to give us space. "And you were in good hands."

Likely, Mom and Daisy and Dad had chased him off. Not like I was in any condition to appreciate his visit then anyway.

Carter reached for me again with his free hand, the cuff of his shirt lifting slightly, the faintest trace of an old scar showing before he made contact. I almost asked him about it before he leaned close and pressed his lips to my forehead, hesitant, as if he wasn't sure if the gesture was welcome. I leaned into the sweet kiss instantly and found myself smiling when he finally pulled away.

"I was thinking," he said, "that maybe the life of a body guard isn't for me anymore. That there might be something a little less demanding and more fulfilling for me to do."

My breath caught at his subtle inference. "You're not going back to L.A.?"

He shrugged, all casual and coy, though with a sparkle of good humor in his eyes. "Hollywood's a big town," he said. "I kind of like the smaller variety. Seems like the people are nicer, you know?"

"If you can get past the bossy mayors, the neighbors who know all your secrets and the murders," I said. "But who's judging?"

He laughed. "I guess." Carter dropped the act, genuine hope in his face. "I'm going to quit. Tonight. Once I'm done here. I'll go see her and tell her I'm done for good." Wow, that was commitment, though I did my best to believe he was doing it for his own good and that it had nothing to do with me because that would be wrong. So wrong. But he obviously meant it, because he stopped referring to her as Ms. Pink. "And I was wondering if you'd object to me looking at maybe settling somewhere close by. Open a small business, maybe."

I couldn't help the hormones, or the big smile that crossed my face. Perhaps I had a thing for Crew, but here was a sweet and caring man who obviously liked me the way I liked him. And was willing to move to my town to see if we could make a go of what we thought could be something.

"Carter," I said, surprised at the hitch in my voice, "I'd really like that." Wow, what a huge gesture. And paused, tried to grasp some semblance of slow down your horses, woman. "What about your family?"

His face darkened just a fraction, gaze dropping to Petunia to who he offered a nice scratch behind her ear, making her moan in happy response. "I'm pretty much on my own," he said. "So making a new home, a new family, is kind of my priority right now. Something that probably won't happen if I stay with the career I'm in."

When Carter met my eyes again, all that wishfulness and gentle sweet nature shining from his expression, I couldn't help myself. I leaned in, lured to that luscious mouth, the warmth of his hand as it settled on my face, how his body curved into mine, his breath passing between my lips.

"Fee!" I know she didn't do it on purpose. I am very much aware my best friend in the entire universe did not just cut off the first kiss I'd had the opportunity to enjoy in months because she was vindictive or jealous. Nor do I believe if she had to do it over again Daisy would have even considered intruding on this very poignant and stirring moment. However.

Yeah.

She gasped as she came to a halt, hand over her mouth, blushing as she stammered an apology. The front door swung shut on its own after her rapid entry, her approach lost in the moment of pending lip connection.

While my bestie tried to backpedal, Carter smiled down at me before standing, helping me to my feet and then saluting Daisy with one hand.

"I'm just glad you're all right," he said. "I'll see you tomorrow?"

I nodded, still in a bit of a daze—thank you adrenaline mixed with painkillers and a concussion—and let him go, not falling back into the couch cushions until the front door shut behind him.

Daisy hurried to me, hugging me as she threw herself down beside me. "Fee, oh my goodness, I'm so sorry, I never, ever would have, not if I'd known. Girl, he's so cute!" She gushed and giggled, then sobered as she sat upright and her face fell. "I'm the worst best friend ever."

"You saved me from making my first kiss a drug-addled choice instead of waiting until I'm fully able to appreciate his hotness." I patted her hand, grinned. "He wants to move here, Daisy." Why did that make me want to giggle like a little girl?

She gasped her delight, hugged me again then retreated with a wince at my hiss of pain. "Sorry again." Daisy's mercurial mood slammed her into shock and then determination. "Crew sent me." She seemed to realize who she mentioned, hesitated. Like

Crew Turner and our lack of dating action was a problem considering the man I'd just almost kissed actually wanted to be with me. I'd deal with my romantic disasters after I was feeling better.

"What does he want now?" It was time for bed. I could feel it, the weight of my weariness, finally enough to knock me out before my addled brain could wire me up for insomnia again.

"It's Willow," she said. "The troopers finally released her, said there wasn't enough evidence and Crew had to stand down. But she was supposed to come back here. She didn't, did she?" Daisy looked over her shoulder as if expecting to see Willow walk down the stairs.

"Not as far as I know," I said.

"I didn't think so. That means she disappeared, Fee, and no one knows where she went."

"Probably back to L.A." But her stuff was still here. While she didn't need any of it, could replace it easily, it didn't seem like her. Unless she was talked into running? "Julian?" That sucked. "Stella?"

But she shook her head as if instinctively understanding the question behind those names. "They are both super worried," she said. "And claim they have nothing to do with her vanishing." Daisy sat back, bit her lower lip. "Crew wants you to stay out of it, naturally. But asked me to let you know. And to tell you that this doesn't look good for her."

It wasn't like she could just disappear. She had a distinctly recognizable face. But yes, I had to admit, running after being released like that? Made her look guilty. Maybe it was time I accepted the fact that Willow Pink killed her husband and played all of us for fools.

The end.

CHAPTER FORTY

THERE WAS NO USE calling Crew. I already knew what he'd say. Still, didn't stop me from fretting and worrying and winding up into the kind of mental state that promised I'd get not one scrap of sleep without more pills.

"I was thinking," Daisy said. Stopped. Shook her head and looked away. "It's stupid."

"I wish you'd stop saying that about yourself." I squeezed her hand. "Say it."

"Well, we might not be able to help Willow," she said. "But I was thinking about what Randy told us about the family. How horrible that was. Maybe we can find something that Willow can use for her defense if the police decide to charge her after all?"

She snorted at her own suggestion. "As if anything justifies murder." She exhaled deeply then perked and slapped her thighs, standing abruptly and offered me her hands while I pondered what she said. "Bed for you, miss."

There was no defense I could think of for murder, though she was rich enough and powerful enough and had a shark like Julian on her side I highly doubted Willow would end up spending any time in prison, even if she was convicted. One sad and tearful admission to a jury about the treatment she endured, his abuse of others and herself, and she'd be back to making movies again.

The likelihood she'd skedaddled back to Hollywood was looking more and more real. And while I didn't want to lose respect for her, I was kind of pissed she'd just run like this. Julian and Stella could claim they had nothing to do with her booking it to the airport until they were purple and aged, but that meant little to me. They'd both do anything to protect her.

I tried not to feel like the woman I thought I was going to be able to call my friend might not be who I'd come to believe she was and sagged into the sofa with a dejected sigh to add to my already wobbly state of mind.

I didn't fight Daisy then when she tugged me to my feet, drifting after her, my pug on my heels. Daisy got my shoes off and tucked me into bed when I protested even bothering getting out of my clothes, feeling a bit grumpy about the whole thing the longer I thought about Willow and her flight from Reading. She didn't even say goodbye. I was being childish and blamed it on the concussion while knowing there was a lot more to it than that.

"I'm not an invalid," I said, taking out my sourness on Daisy.

"Will you please just let me help you?" She wrinkled her nose, handed me a pill from the prescription bottle and the glass of water. I shook my head, sinking into the pillows, refusing the comfort the painkillers could offer. No more drugs. I'd rather suffer with a sore head than fall down that rabbit hole. Besides, they left a bad taste in my mouth in more ways than one.

Daisy turned off the light and closed my door over, leaving me with my pug to circle and fret and grunt as she tried to find a place that worked for her. It took a long time for her to settle after Daisy left and I finally got out of bed with a cranky growl at her in search of entertainment if she was going to insist on keeping me awake.

My best friend wasn't in the living room, but my laptop was. The idea of a movie appealed so I brought it back to bed with me, bare feet padding on the soft carpet, the covers warm and welcoming as I settled in next to Petunia who finally found the perfect place to lie down, her chin on my pillow. Naturally.

"Let's see if we can find something to knock us out," I said to her. She groaned her agreement.

But, instead, as my fingers hovered, the search engine screen waiting for my input, I had a thought. And tapped Randy Russell's name in to the bar before hitting enter.

A moment later, Petunia with her chin now transferred to my shoulder, gazing at the bright screen with her bulging eyes, I scanned articles about the death and subsequent scandal surrounding Skip and Jason that seemed to have been rapidly and utterly swept under the rug. Interesting to read Randy's blog and the story he told us in his written word, how his primary focus, it appeared, was Skip Anderson and no other topic. When he set out for revenge, he didn't take prisoners. I would have thought there was enough in the way of chatter, pictures and even the odd video of Skip abusing people verbally, taking drugs and drinking far too much that the team must have seen the writing on the wall. Which was maybe what turned Jason's death and this last concussion into the icing on Skip's thanks but you're fired cake.

I scrolled past the text in the latest article before spotting an image I hadn't seen yet on the sidebar, squinting past my dizziness to read the date. When I clicked on it, the photo of a young football player in the prime of his budding career appeared, smiling for the camera, his dark eyes seeming to lock on mine.

My entire body went cold, muscles spasming with surprise so powerful I locked up a moment. I gasped loudly enough at the sight of Jason Hagan Petunia barked and farted in rapid succession, leaping back from me like I'd scared her.

Instead of comforting her, I pushed my laptop aside and lunged for my phone. Too fast, Fee, slow down. A dizzy spell washed over me, nausea powerfully commanding, forcing me to lie over the edge of the bed, all the blood rushing to my head as I salivated heavily and swallowed down the bile threatening to emerge while I panted and prayed for it to end.

By the time the wave of sickness passed I was able to roll back over and stared up into Petunia's worried, bulging eyes, my heart pounding, entire body slick with a cold sweat.

"That was dumb," I whispered to her.

Two pills went down once I fumbled them from the bottle, a wash of water as I got out of bed at last and headed for the kitchen, dialing Crew on my way to the stairs. I'm not sure why I felt the need to go up to the main house. I wasn't actually going to see him, just calling him, but moving toward him in a general kind of way helped steady my pulse like nothing else.

Four rings buzzed in my ear before his answering service picked up. I swore softly as I paused halfway to the top of the stairs and tried again. This time the call went right to voicemail and I knew he was ignoring me on purpose.

Damn him, of all times to cut me off when I knew who the murderer was.

Okay, fine. Dad. But I had to find Willow first, and fast. Because if I was right, she hadn't run for the hills, was nowhere near L.A. and it was very likely her life was in danger. I was sure of it. Had a hint of it earlier, didn't I? When the person who killed Skip told me he was going to quit his job later that night. Tell Willow in person.

Olivia answered on the first ring. "Fiona." She sounded flustered.

"Just shut up and tell me where Willow is." I didn't have time for her crap.

"How am I supposed to know?" She didn't get to go on, someone fighting her for her phone before Stella came on. "What's wrong? You know where Willow went?"

Her fear sounded real. "Get to Crew Turner right now," I said. "Tell him to arrest Carter Melnick. And find Willow. I think he's going to try to kill her tonight."

I paused at the kitchen door, the entry already half swung open, and froze as Stella chattered in my head. Dropped my phone, heard Petunia yip and didn't even look down to see if I'd hit her with it. Because I wasn't alone.

"Very good, Fee," Carter said, Willow in a headlock against him, a needle pressed to her throat. "But I wish you hadn't made that call."

CHAPTER FORTY-ONE

I STARED AT THE pair of them, Willow ever so pale, Carter's handsome face as kind and worried as I'd ever seen it. And those eyes, those beautiful dark eyes of his.

"Your brother had your eyes," I said. Maybe a silly thing to blurt out while he held his former employer at needlepoint and what had to be a lethal dose of Quexol in the barrel.

"I guess he did," he said. "But Jay was a hundred times the man I ever was." His face crumpled, moisture forming in his lashes. "I was a waste of space from day one, never made anything of myself. Got into drugs and petty crime while he set his heart on football. And he made it, Fee." That smile. I'd fallen for the curve of it, the gentleness behind it. How had I misread him so badly? "He was making something of himself."

"Carter." Willow choked out his name. "I'm so sorry about your brother."

It was the very first time I saw the man he used to be. Or maybe the man he still was, honestly, hidden behind a façade of polished professionalism. A flare of utter rage like a bursting volcano, a shift in stance barely noticeable, a flash of energy so intense she cried out though he didn't visibly hurt her in any way.

"Shut. Up." This was the Carter who killed Skip, I guess. The Carter—if that was even his name—who almost killed himself getting high on a regular basis. He met my gaze again, the rage draining out of him, and shrugged a little, the end of the needle pricking her thin skin, making a dent in her flesh. It had to have gone in. And her jugular pulsed beneath it. "I wasn't talking to you, Ms. Pink. I was talking to Fee."

Her huge eyes begged me to do something. But I could barely focus, let alone act. My head throbbed, though from the concussion or my own self-doubt I couldn't tell.

Carter spoke before I could come up with a single thing to say that wouldn't emerge in an incoherent gurgle. "I thought I could trust you." He looked away a moment, lips thinning to a disappointed line. "I thought we had something special to build on, Fee. I guess I was wrong."

"Carter," I whispered. "You tried to kill me." Forget Skip Anderson. Screw that asshole. Carter hit me with the handle of my own damned shovel and almost took my head off. Anger built, and I know it had to show on my face, because his own, rather than going hard and furious, reflected his regret.

"I'm so sorry," he said. "I never meant to hurt you, I swear. I had to shut him up."

"Who?" I realized then I already had that answer. "Randy."

He nodded while Willow shifted ever so slightly in his grip. Did he feel her movement, the way she settled her weight in his hands? I saw it, tried to ignore it, was grateful he was locked on me and not her at the moment and hoped I didn't give her away in my screwed up state.

Then again, what exactly did she have planned that wasn't going to end up with her dying of an overdose and me likely bludgeoned to death by the man I thought I could fall in love and share my life with?

"Russell knew me," he said then. "I did my best to avoid him, keep my head down. He never made the connection, but he was clever. And I figured the longer this wound out, the more chance he had of recognizing me." Carter smiled, tremulous and sad. "You're right, by the way. I do have the same eyes. But thankfully Jay took after Mom and I look enough like my father I got away with it."

"Almost did, you mean," I said. "Would have, Carter. If you'd just let Willow go." Then again, I guess I proved that wasn't the case. But he could have run, could have hid himself away in the old life he used to live and no one would have found him, I was positive of that.

"How could I?" His hands shook, the needle trembling where it pricked Willow's skin. She sagged further, eyes never leaving me, though he didn't seem to notice. "It was as much her fault as his. She just let him do it, didn't argue, didn't fight. And, in the end, it was her lawyer who advised Skip to settle."

Willow gasped softly. "You weren't there." She seemed suddenly ashamed and I was glad. "You can't know that."

"Paulie told me," he said. "Your favorite body guard." The one that disappeared? Carter said one vanished and he got the job thanks to the temp agency. "Right before I killed him." Oh my god. "Funny thing, this was only about Skip, you know. To that point you weren't even on my radar. I was going to let you live." He whispered that admission into her ear. "Until you took part in their plan to screw over my parents. And then you had to go, too."

My mind flashed to the carriage and Skip's slip, disjointed thoughts coming together in a rush.

"You drugged him out on the street," I said. "Right in front of everyone."

Carter nodded to me, though he didn't seem happy or proud of his success. "He was so wasted by then I decided to chance it. I was going to wait and dose them both later, make it look like a murder suicide, like he'd finally snapped. But he just pissed me off so much, Fee. And I couldn't resist." He shook his head, looked down at Willow's face beneath his, arm tight around her neck. "A mistake. I should have had more restraint and they'd both be dead and I wouldn't have to kill you, too." He met my gaze as he finished, chill washing down my spine at his sad and yet casual admission.

"You know, plotting to kill them was the motivation I needed to get clean. Ironic, right?" That chuckle, so gentle, so Carter. "I stopped cold turkey the day Mom died, swore I'd make them pay. Started eating healthy, gained weight. Found out it was easy to get a job as a bodyguard with my old looks still intact."

The scar on his wrist, his long sleeved shirt and jacket he was never without. "You worked hard to hide who you were." And not just his identity, but the person he used to be.

"Easier than I thought," he said. "I used my middle name and my mother's maiden one, her dead brother's social security number and Joey Hagan was dead in a fire in a squat and Carter Melnick was born."

Did he burn down that house with those people inside? I decided I didn't want to know.

"That was a lucky break," he said like he knew what I was thinking and needed to tell me everything. "Already in progress when I got there. So I took advantage and dumped my old life and never looked back."

Okay then. Yes, he'd killed the body guard and Skip, but at least he didn't burn three drug addicts or street people or whoever they were alive. Guy had some sense of honor. Except he didn't try to help them either, did he?

Fee. I needed more drugs.

"It wasn't supposed to end this way," Carter said. "I was supposed to take them both out at the same time and disappear, and no one would ever know it was me. I'd find somewhere to hide, live out the rest of my life and do good, in Jay's name." There wasn't much I could say to that. Because he honestly believed he'd done the right thing. Carter cleared his throat, his face settling into a mask of cold determination. "I should have known better than to come back, but I wanted to see you one last time. I should have just killed her and run."

"You planted the syringe and bottle in the third floor bathroom to implicate Evelyn," I said. "Then the one under Willow's bed after Crew and Dad already searched to make sure we thought it was her."

He shrugged. "Pathetic. I was pretty sure at that point she'd get off, so I had to try." Carter twitched ever so slightly, regretfully. "This is a mess, and I'm sorry you're going to suffer for it, Fee. But I can't let you go. You have to know that."

"I didn't do anything to your brother," I said. "Carter, you can turn yourself in. Skip's dead. It doesn't have to end this way."

I had to try. But my usual persuasiveness was obviously defective thanks to the concussion or the drugs or my weakness. Regardless the reason, he looked away from me, body tensing as he prepared to inject Willow with the contents of the syringe.

"Say goodbye, Ms. Pink," he said.

As Willow collapsed utterly, one foot lashing out to impact his knee and dragging him down to the floor with her.

CHAPTER FORTY-TWO

I LEAPED TOWARD THE pair without thinking, head blazing with pain I fought to ignore, and landed on the two of them like some kind of ridiculous superhero who'd lost her cape along the way. My fingers skittered for the syringe, impacting Carter's hand and tearing at the plastic tube. While my intentions were good, my aim was off, my own grasp too slow to save the day while Carter fumbled the prize. It went flying across the tile despite my efforts to nab it, spinning until it came to a halt against the side of the fridge. Carter grunted under my weight, Willow squirming beside me, her slim body writhing for purchase and leverage.

Well, at least he didn't have possession of the deadly weapon anymore, either.

There should have been shouting or cursing or some kind of noise aside from the anxious yips of my pug as she circled and tried to get to me. But the three of us struggled in near silence, only the soft moan of my pain escaping my lips when I tried to pin Carter's arms, his faint grunts when he shifted sideways to slip out from under me, Willow's gasping breath while she lashed out with both feet, trying to kick him hard enough to incapacitate him.

Such silence held more weight than stone and I felt my breath stolen from my chest, terror rising like a tide inside me, swallowing my courage and reducing me to an animal like state while I bit and punched and grappled with the man I knew, if we let him up, would kill both of us.

In the end, it was Willow who took care of our assailant, gaining her knees while I wriggled and fought to keep Carter pinned, landing hard on my side when his superior strength bucked me off. I rolled over, ready to throw up from the nausea and agony, to see the starlet hit him hard in the sternum then undercut his jaw before round house kicking him in the side of the head.

He spun toward me as he went down, eyes rolling back into his head and collapsed on his face while Willow sprang to her feet, bouncing on her toes and I was grateful—oh so grateful—she learned to do her own stunts.

Willow hurried to me, tried to help me up. "Fee, are you all right?"

Petunia chuffed as I shook and did my best not to cry, her words sounding so loud after the quiet intensity of the fight. "You're awesome," I said.

She didn't get to respond. Petunia barked once sharply and I gasped at her, breathless still, tried to warn Willow but too late, as Carter lurched upright. Petunia barked again and Willow spun, taking Carter's fist to her face. Her turn to go down, twisting sideways from the blow's momentum while I scrambled, stomach heaving, back away from him.

Slow motion never felt so much like a horror movie. Nothing seemed to gain me the kind of control I needed, pushing with both feet across the tile, trying for purchase and failing to stand. Skidding like I was in a pool of cold molasses, caught in the grasp of desperation for speed and unable to find it. When my back hit the fridge, the hum of the big stainless steel appliance vibrated between my shoulder blades like a warning I didn't need as time wound down toward the tick-tick-tick of infinitesimal anticipation of the end.

Carter approached slowly, face twisting into something I didn't recognize while my mouth dropped open and a scream finally escaped. Petunia skirted him but stayed out of his way, smart pug, and I prayed once I was gone he'd leave her alone. Just don't kill my dog, I beg you. I think I actually said it, the last word trailing out of me in a whisper as the shriek of my terror died in my mouth.

My heart pounded so loud I couldn't hear anything after that, had to force air into my lungs, my head the one shrieking now, pain overwhelming me, hands grasping at the tile under me for a weapon, the means to fight, anything, anything at all to keep him away and not let this end how I knew it had to.

Even as my fingertips found plastic and steel.

I froze, the syringe in my hand suddenly, time turning forward so fast I was numbed by its return to normal. Hands hidden behind one hip, I waited, the hardest thing I'd ever done in my life. My world was Carter, a black tunnel of focus leading only to him as he finally kicked Petunia away and lunged for me, hands reaching for my neck.

And then I was choking, his grip cutting off my air, instantly and with a hideously agonized look on his face.

The kind of look you remember for the rest of your life. Especially if it was about to be over.

I knew my arm moved, and I knew my thumb found the plunger. I didn't know, though, not then, if I'd managed to inject him somewhere that I'd make a difference. If the drug could possibly take him down in time to save my life. And as the darkness closed in, my breath cut off, to the distant sound of Petunia barking and barking, I figured I wouldn't live to find out after all.

There was light and air when I was sure none would ever return and I was coughing, someone pulling Carter away from me, the sound of a fist impacting a face, and Crew stood over me, the now fully unconscious murderer at his feet while I clasped at my aching throat, my throbbing head, and wept in relief.

Crew crouched next to me, pulling me against his chest while the kitchen flooded with people.

"My hero," I managed through tearing sobs.

"You first," he whispered.

I would have liked to answer. But as the weight of what happened slammed into me, weeping making breathing a chore, the darkness called for real and I wasn't in a position to fight its call anymore.

CHAPTER FORTY-THREE

ILLOW SIPPED HER TEA, one long, thin leg folded elegantly over the other, her skinny jeans ripped at the knee. She'd made no effort to hide her split lip or the bruise forming from Carter's knockout punch, instead letting the truth show like she wore it proudly. She set her cup in her saucer and exhaled the scent of chamomile, the breeze carrying it to me while I stared into my coffee and just enjoyed her company.

Hard to believe we'd fought for our lives just last night. That it was time to say goodbye, that this woman I'd come to adore and admire was leaving Reading and I'd likely not see her again for a long time. If ever. Because we hardly traveled in the same circles. But I was glad to see the smile she shared, most of the weariness gone from her face.

"Thank you, Fee," she said, patting my hand with fingers warmed by her tea. "This means a lot to me. Just sitting. I don't get to be quiet much."

"Maybe you should make it a habit more often." I looked up into the spring sunlight and noted the clouds gathering in the distance. There was a chill to the breeze that felt like snow. So maybe we were in for a late storm and the ski hill would get a reprieve after all.

"I'm thinking I should make visiting Reading a habit." She patted Petunia's wrinkled head. "I'd love to come home to my friends." She seemed so shy when she said it, as if she didn't think she'd be welcome after all. And, I suppose, she had good reason to hesitate. We hadn't exactly had the best introduction.

I smiled back at her. "Any time," I said. "I mean that."

Willow sighed. "I still have an obligation to fill for Olivia. We're doing a quick film session this afternoon."

She *what?* Wow, she was a bigger woman than me, that was for sure.

"Then back to L.A.?" Life would be so different without Skip. I wondered if she'd be happy at last. Or would she somehow turn him into a martyr in her mind and miss him regardless of the man he became?

"I have a contract," she said. "A new action movie. I've been practicing my fighting." She laughed shakily. "But you know that."

"And I'm very grateful for it." I sipped some coffee. "You saved our lives."

"I think it was a team effort." Willow stood then, Julian appearing at the back door, gesturing to her but ignoring me so I guess nothing really changed in his mind. "I'll text you?"

We hugged and she left, the kitchen door closing behind her. And then, it opened again, and the cranky lawyer/manager poked his well-groomed head out and nodded to me before disappearing again.

So something had changed then. Good to know.

I was about to go inside, wishing I had a thicker sweater, when Pamela appeared through the kitchen door. I waved for her to join me, settled in for her visit, while she tentatively sank down next to me.

"You look like crap, Fee," she said.

Nice. "I've had a rough day or so."

She snorted a laugh, leaned back. "I don't know if it was you or not," she said, "but Willow Pink just agreed to give me an exclusive interview about what happened." She didn't look at me, seemed acutely interested in the bush starting to bloom beside her. "What do you think of that?"

I just grinned. Wasn't me. But let her wonder.

"From what I understand," she said then, "you've made a fan out of Mila Martin."

That didn't sound promising. "What do you mean?"

"Not sure," Pamela said, patting my knee. "But if her obsessive nature with Willow wasn't a warning, you might want to consider hiring a bodyguard of your own."

Great. Just what I needed. "Whatever," I said. "I'm not that exciting. She'll get bored soon enough."

Pamela didn't answer and I had a sick feeling I hadn't seen the last of Mila.

My kitchen had turned into a revolving door, it seemed, Pamela's cheery exit after delivering that not-so-happy information followed rapidly by Crew's turn at the Fee carousel. I'd already had to hug my mother three times, promise Daisy I would go to bed before five, endure my father's long, mournful stares he pretended weren't anything important and the silent treatment of the horrified and guilty Jones sisters. The last person I expected, though, was Crew Turner looking hangdog with a bouquet of flowers in one hand and his hat in the other.

Quite frankly, I was happy to see him. At least he wasn't Olivia. I hadn't endured that particular visit yet and wondered if it would ever happen. Didn't matter now, not while the handsome sheriff of Curtis County hesitantly offered me the spring mix before sinking awkwardly to the bench beside me where Willow and Pamela had taken turns.

"I meant to give you those at the hospital." He gestured at the lovely bunch with his hat, face tentative, hands shaking a little. "Terri made them up special for you. When she heard, you know." He cleared his throat, obviously uncomfortable.

"She's doing well, then?" She'd kept the flower store herself, kicking her gambling and drug addict husband, Simon Jacob, out of the picture and taking a firm grasp on her own life. I was pretty proud of her for it, too.

"Seems to be." Crew nodded, coughed softly again like something had caught in his throat. "You're doing better?"

It was kind of a dumb question, but he was trying. I thought of Mom and her suggestion before answering. "Yes, thanks," I said. Choked up a bit myself though I hadn't meant to. "For everything, Crew."

"You didn't need me." He stared at the ground between his feet. "Doc said that shot you gave Melnick was just about to kick in before I got there. Somehow you hit a vein and he was already on his way down." Crew laughed a little, but without humor. "You're a walking disaster waiting to happen, Fiona Fleming, but you're damned good at saving yourself, too, aren't you?"

I shrugged. "Is that a problem?" What a weird conversation to be having in the spring sunshine.

Crew looked up, startled, met my eyes. "Actually," he said, a slow smile creeping across his face, making him look like a little kid for a second, "that's my favorite."

I giggled at his expression. "You like women who get themselves in trouble and then fish themselves back out again? What, are you a sucker for punishment?"

Crew's grin softened and his gaze grew distant. "I guess I must be," he said. "Did I ever tell you about my wife?"

Wait, what? He was married? No ring. I spluttered internally while he went on as if I'd answered anyway.

"You remind me of her in a lot of ways," he said, voice quiet, deep. The clouds closed in around the sun for a moment, casting us both in shadow and chilling me with the loss of warmth. "She had your kind of willful courage, threw herself into things that most people wouldn't even think to try." His smile was soft, sad. "I loved her for that."

I didn't have to ask despite always wondering what his story was about. Knowing then it wasn't divorce that parted them. "How did she die?"

"Cancer." He shrugged like it was the expected answer. "Two years ago." Crew's fingers spun his hat in his hands. "I came to Reading from Berkley because I didn't want to be on the West coast anymore. It reminded me too much of her. And because when my dad died, he made me promise I'd come here someday. Make it my home."

How odd. For the second time, I noted the anchor and skull on his left wrist, the tattoo with the off center compass, North facing, not at his palm, but somewhere into the distance. Like he was looking for something and that arrow pointed the way.

"I'm sorry, Crew." I touched his arm, then held his hand as he offered it to me.

"So, here goes, then," he said, all brusque and nervous again. "It's been two years since I dated anyone and I never really wanted to after Michelle died. But she didn't want me to be alone and I told her when I was ready I'd try again."

Wait, ready for what?

Crew must have seen the startled look in my eyes because he laughed then, squeezed my hand.

"I'm not asking you to marry me, Fee," he said, a twinkle in his gaze.

"Well, you kind of propositioned me the other night already," I said with a cheeky grin. "So I wasn't sure what kind of speed you're accustomed to, California boy."

That cut the last of the tension and relaxed him to the point he settled back on the bench.

"I'm not ready," he said, as if admitting that hurt a lot. "But when I am, Fee. I think... if you're willing to consider it?"

My heart cracked, wept as I continued to smile for the genuine hope in his eyes. Remembered hope in another man's gaze not so long ago and wondered if I could trust my own feelings ever again. And nodded to Crew.

"You come see me," I said. "And we'll talk about it."

Crew exhaled softly. "If you're still free."

"If I'm still alive." I softened that with a wink.

We both laughed. But without real amusement. Because honestly? Just not as funny out loud as it had been in my head. For the time being, though, sitting there as the sun broke through again and the clouds vanished over the mountain, dumping their white goodness on the towering heights, I was happy just to hold Crew Turner's hand.

CHAPTER FORTY-FOUR

I SORTED THROUGH THE last of the reservations and sighed as I stepped back from the sidebar in the foyer, rubbing my tired eyes and wondering how it had been a week already since Carter Melnick was arrested for the murder of Skip Anderson.

He was out of the hospital, awaiting arraignment, according to Crew. They'd intervened in time to save him from an overdose, so at least I didn't have his death on my hands. But the remnants of his attack would linger for months, I figured, though Dr. Aberstock was happy with my recovery rate despite the fact I refused to just sit on my ass and feel it get wider while my parents, staff and best friend did all the work for me.

Tomorrow marked the arrival of my first guests since I vacated the Johansens from the Blue Suite thanks to Olivia. Who, naturally, had avoided me like the plague since Carter was arrested. I would track her down at some point and force her to admit she owed me a giant one that far surpassed anything she did to keep Petunia's open when Pete Wilkins died in my koi pond. But, for now, I was happy to organize the insanity that was coming and do my best to keep my energy up and not push so hard I had to hand the reins to someone else.

Petunia's was my place, now more than ever, and I loved it.

"You're sure you don't need me to stay for the season?" Daisy joined me from the kitchen, her hands full of mail. She'd fretted over the decision all week, but I insisted she go despite knowing I could use her. Mom and Dad already offered and I'd rather she found her own path, thank you.

"Pat and Ashley would be devastated if you didn't give it a go." The local real estate husband and wife team had happily accepted Daisy as a trainee and I loved the glow in her eyes when she talked about all the ins and outs she was learning. Sales of new homes were booming so it was a great time for her to get into business with the Champvilles.

"You call me if you need anything." She set the mail down on the sidebar, envelopes settling on top of the most current *Reading Reader Gazette*. They covered the mug shot of Carter, the long and detailed article about the murder just as well hidden. While Pamela wrote a glowing story about Willow and—to my embarrassment and chagrin—me, I'd had enough of the past and was just as happy to turn my mind forward.

Daisy didn't seem to notice the favor she'd done me, instead handing me her final burden, a medium sized cardboard box. "From New York?"

I frowned down at it before reading the return label and gasped a soft and excited sound, reaching for the letter opener. Daisy grinned though I hadn't explained and waited while I cut the tape and opened the seal, pushing the packing peanuts out of the way and lifting free the music box my grandmother left me.

The trail of clues—from the buried metal box in the backyard to the safety deposit key, to this very treasure—had led me to this moment and I could barely contain my excitement.

Daisy helped herself to the folded letter inside and read it out loud as I hugged the gold and red velvet to my chest a moment.

"Dear Miss Fleming," she read, "please find enclosed the music box you requested repaired. While we were happy to do a general cleaning and attempt to fix the mechanism, it's with sadness we admit defeat. Mr. Burrow, our specialist, passed away last year and without his expertise, we were unable to complete the job. We have only billed you for partial work and hope you find someone who can finish what we started. Our very best, Clingman and Sons Fine Jewelers."

How disappointing. I felt my heart drop with every word and finally released the box, setting it on the sideboard and looking at it in mournful regret.

"Oh Fee," Daisy said, sorrow in her own voice. "I'm sorry. I love that music box. What's wrong with it?"

"It won't play." I shrugged, fighting the same tears I'd felt the day I recovered it from the bank. It had taken a week to find someone who thought they could fix it and they'd had it for a month and a half now. This disappointment, coming on the heels of the recent past, was almost more than I could take.

But Daisy wasn't about to let me down. She beamed at me, reached for it while I had to hold myself back from taking it away from her in a surge of the gimmies. *Mine*, shrieked in my head while she carefully opened the lid then wound the key on the back. Again those three familiar notes played before dying off. Still broken. Then, Daisy winked and turned the key back a whole turn.

The ballerina spun as the music began to play, the tinkling loveliness of it piercing my heart with memory. She set it on the side board again and held my hand while we listened to its merry tune, and I found myself humming along in utter delight, hugging her abruptly when the music was over.

"Daisy," I breathed into her hair. "How?"

"Iris showed me once," she said, wiping at tears in her eyes though we both grinned like kids at each other. "There was a trick to it."

Obviously. I turned back to the box, delighted this story had a happy ending. And froze.

The front of the box had clicked open, a small drawer in evidence. Daisy frowned, shook her head with her eyebrows rising when I glanced at her in curiosity.

"I've never seen it do that before," she said.

With trembling fingers, I opened the drawer further, peeking inside. Gasped in surprise.

A scrap of some kind of old parchment lay within. I pulled it out, pinching the corner with my fingernails, though not sure why I felt the need to be so careful. It was rough on one edge, torn on the other, as if part of a bigger something ripped away. The side showing was blank, but when I flipped it over, Daisy squeaked and reached for it while I gaped at the name Reading written in flowing ink and the half a compass, the North pointing off to the left, torn down the middle.

"Fee." Daisy looked up, met my eyes, hers full of wonder. "This can't be what I think it is."

The little drawer wasn't empty just yet. I reached in and this time, when I pulled out the contents, I almost dropped the round, heavy coin. Not because it was slippery or gold or even out of clumsiness. But because I'd seen one like it before.

"That's." Daisy stopped abruptly.

"A doubloon." I swallowed hard.

"Fee." She squealed my name, grasping my arm and shaking me, the coin bouncing in my palm. You know what this means?"

The Reading Hoard. The treasure of Captain William Reading, the same man whose statue I'd mocked in disbelief, Olivia's next step in promoting our town. The privateer who founded this very place I called home. All this time the legend had been treated like a fairy tale. Even the occasional hunters who'd come to look had left empty handed after a short sniff around, as if the unbelievable story really wasn't true.

But, if these pieces left for me meant what I thought they meant...

The treasure was real. And Grandmother Iris didn't just know that. She wanted me to go looking for it.

The Reading
Reader Gazette

VOLUME 1 ISSUE 1 — APRIL 12TH, 2018 — WWW.RRGAZETTE.COM

News Briefs

1. **Yacht Club Seeks Designs:** In conjunction with Reading Town Council, the Reading Yacht Club is looking for design options for next year's Captain Reading's Pirate Horde celebration to be held during July and August. Please note, all designs must be tasteful and reflect the existing branding the town council has chosen. All submissions due by July 31st to the club office.

2. **Parking Violations:** Your town council would like to remind you that parking restrictions for the tourist season begin on May 30th and will continue until September 1st. Any Reading resident whose vehicle is found parked outside their driveway or on town property, taking up valuable parking space for visitors, will be towed at their expense. Let's keep Reading's streets open for our tourists!

3. **Easter Egg Hunt Rescheduled:** Please note, this year's egg hunt at town hall has been rescheduled at last to next weekend to avoid any issues arising from the filming of the new commercial. Parents and children are advised to arrive early for a chance for photos with the Easter Bunny himself! (One photo per child.)

4. **Missing Angel:** Could whoever borrowed the angel statue from the Contemplation Park at First Christian Church please return it. No questions asked, your reasons are your own. Besides, you'll answer to the Lord when the time comes. He's a better judge than we are.

Winner of this week's Fire Hall 50/50 draw: Lucy Fleming. Congratulations, Lucy!

Please send any pending community notices to: pamela@rrgazette.com before 4PM.

Fame Can Be Murder

Carter Melnick, brother of deceased football hopeful Jason Hagan, has been arrested for the murder of Reading native Skip Anderson and the attempted murder of Ms. Willow Pink and Petunia's owner Ms. Fiona Fleming.

Revenge is served hot during the warmest April on record

By Pamela Shard

In a drug haze of painkillers and alcohol, Skip Anderson, 27, died horribly at the hands of the vengeful family member of football rising star, Jason Hagan, 20, of New Jersey. Tragically, the young football player took his own life after a terrible accident destroyed his chance to play the game he loved. Blaming Anderson for the deaths of his brother and that of his mother of a heart attack shortly after, Carter Melnick, 31, administered a lethal dose of experimental painkiller into Anderson, killing him soon after.

Thanks to the hard work of our own local sheriff's department, and with the help of former Curtis County Sheriff John Fleming and his daughter, Fiona Fleming, Melnick's attempt to frame Anderson's wife, Hollywood star and local legend, Willow Pink, ended in his arrest, though not before he attacked both Ms Pink and Ms. Fleming with the intent to kill them both to protect himself from prosecution.

"I wouldn't be here if it weren't for the bravery and consistent police work of Sheriff Turner, former Sheriff Fleming, and Fiona Fleming," Ms. Pink said. "Their commitment to clearing my name and finding the real killer led to this arrest and justice for Skip."

The West Coast Whales were unavailable for comment, but coach Matt Almeda, former personal coach to Anderson, told us he was saddened by the deaths of both young football players and hopes that this might serve to bring awareness to both the impact of injury on athletes and the excessive use of painkillers in his sport.

When asked about the rumor Anderson had actually chosen to cancel his contract with Reading and that the plan to use his fame to promote our town further had been shut down, Mayor Olivia Walker assures us that isn't the case.

"Ms. Pink is a joy to work with and we're thrilled to have her be the face of Reading. Hopefully for many years to come."

Meanwhile, Reading's popularity with tourists

COMING SOON, THE NEXT in the Fiona
Fleming Cozy Mysteries series...

FIONA FLEMING COZY MYSTERIES #4

GHOSTS AND GOBLINS AND

MURDER

PATTI LARSEN

AUTHOR NOTES

I'M HAVING SO MUCH fun.

So much. More than I ever expected I would. Every time I think about Fiona's books I get excited, pumped up, giggly and feel like I've found the thing that wakes me up in the morning.

Yes, I love to write, and all of the voices are special to me. Including my beloved Ethie. But there's something truly delicious about all of this I'm just tickled to dive into.

But, it's time to step away from her, just for a little bit. Some updates are due you because I know you'll be looking for them. I've been writing and publishing steadily since mid-January. With the release of *The Forsaken* (**The Hayle Coven Inheritance**) the end of March, I'll have released five new books this year already and I'm not slowing down even a bit.

However, the next month or so will be dedicated to projects I've promised others and that aren't Fiona or Syd or any of the other voices you've come to love.

I have the launch of the **Lovely Witches Club webseries** coming in May and need to complete the other six novelettes, as well as two books for boxed sets due in the next few months (both of which I think you'll love, so stay tuned!) and a very special young woman has waited patiently for me to finally finish the **Adventures of Susan and Tucker** (*Cat City* has been out for almost eight years and the sequels deserve to be written). I'll be tackling those as well, while trying to fit in book four of this series, *Ghosts and Goblins and Murder.*

Don't worry, I'm hard at it and you'll have something familiar at least once a month! But if I disappear, please know I'm working, just on things you may not get to see until August or September. Exciting things that hopefully will spark something new... we'll see!

For now, thank you for reading, as always, and have a magical day,

Patti

ABOUT THE AUTHOR

EVERYTHING YOU NEED TO know about me is in this one statement: I've wanted to be a writer since I was a little girl, and now I'm doing it. How cool is that, being able to follow your dream and make it reality? I've tried everything from university to college, graduating the second with a journalism diploma (I sucked at telling real stories), was in an all-girl improv troupe for five glorious years (if you've never tried it, I highly recommend making things up as you go along as often as possible). I've even been in a Celtic girl band (some of our stuff is on YouTube!) and was an independent film maker. My life has been one creative thing after another—all leading me here, to writing books for a living.

Now with multiple series in happy publication, I live on beautiful and magical Prince Edward Island (I know you've heard of Anne of Green Gables) with my very patient husband and six massive cats.

I love-love-love hearing from you! You can reach me (and I promise I'll message back) at patti@pattilarsen.com. And if you're eager for your next dose of Patti Larsen books (usually about one release a month) come join my mailing list! All the best up and coming, giveaways, contests and, of course, my observations on the world (aren't you just dying to know what I think about everything?) all in one place: http://smarturl.it/PattiLarsenEmail.

Last—but not least!—I hope you enjoyed what you read! Your happiness is my happiness. And I'd love to hear just what you thought. **A review** where you found this book would mean the world to me— **reviews feed writers** more than you will ever know. So, loved it (or not so much), **your honest review** would make my day. **Thank you!**

Made in the USA
Lexington, KY
10 May 2018